FUN學
美國英語閱讀課本
各學科實用課文 二版

+ Workbook

AMERICAN
SCHOOL
TEXTBOOK
READING KEY

作者 Michael A. Putlack & e-Creative Contents　　譯者 丁宥暄

MP3
寂天雲 APP

如何下載 MP3 音檔

❶ 寂天雲 APP 聆聽：掃描書上 QR Code 下載「寂天雲－英日語學習隨身聽」APP。加入會員後，用 APP 內建掃描器再次掃描書上 QR Code，即可使用 APP 聆聽音檔。

❷ 官網下載音檔：請上「寂天閱讀網」（www.icosmos.com.tw），註冊會員／登入後，搜尋本書，進入本書頁面，點選「MP3 下載」下載音檔，存於電腦等其他播放器聆聽使用。

American School Textbook
Reading Key

The Best Preparation for Building Academic Reading Skills and Vocabulary

The Reading Key series is designed to help students to understand American school textbooks and to develop background knowledge in a wide variety of academic topics. This series also provides learners with the opportunity to enhance their reading comprehension skills and vocabulary, which will assist them when they take various English exams.

Reading Key <Volume 1-3> is
a three-book series designed for beginner to intermediate learners.

Reading Key <Volume 4-6> is
a three-book series designed for intermediate to high-intermediate learners.

Reading Key <Volume 7-9> is
a three-book series designed for high-intermediate learners.

Features

- A wide variety of topics that cover American school subjects
  helps learners expand their knowledge of academic topics through interdisciplinary studies

- Intensive practice for reading skill development
  helps learners prepare for various English exams

- Building vocabulary by school subjects and themed texts
  helps learners expand their vocabulary and reading skills in each subject

- Graphic organizers for each passage
  show the structure of the passage and help to build summary skills

- Captivating pictures and illustrations related to the topics
  help learners gain a broader understanding of the topics and key concepts

Table of Contents

Workbook for Daily Review

Syllabus Vol. 1

Subject	Topic & Area	Title
Social Studies ★ **History and Geography**	School Life	Our Day at School
	School Life	School Rules
	Citizenship	Welcome to My Community
	Citizenship	Being a Good Citizen
	Culture	Celebrating Holidays
	Culture	Holiday Traditions
	National Symbols	America's Symbols
	National Symbols	National Flags
	Government	America's Capital
	Government	Washington, D.C.
	Geography	Our Land and Water
	Geography	Where in the World Do We Live?
Science	A World of Plants	Parts of Plants
	A World of Plants	What Do Plants Need?
	Animals and Their Homes	Where Do Animals Live?
	Animals and Their Homes	Water Habitats
	Weather and Seasons	Weather
	Weather and Seasons	The Four Seasons
	The Solar System	What Can You See in the Sky?
	The Solar System	What Causes Day and Night?
	Changes in Matter	Solids, Liquids, and Gases
	Changes in Matter	The Water Cycle
	The Human Body	Your Body
	The Human Body	The Systems of Your Body
Mathematics	Geometry	Shapes and Figures
	Geometry	What Am I?
	Numbers and Counting	Counting Numbers
	Numbers and Counting	Comparing Numbers
Language and Literature	Language Arts	Language Arts
	Language Arts	Language Arts
	Types of Writing	Reading Stories
	Reading Stories	Reading Stories
Visual Arts	A World of Paintings	Kinds of Paintings
	A World of Paintings	Painting and Drawing Materials
Music	A World of Music	Musical Instruments
	A World of Music	The Orchestra

1

- **Social Studies**
- **History and Geography**

Key Words

- activity
- show respect
- flag
- face
- Pledge of Allegiance
- subject
- solve
- classmate
- get along

We go to school each day.
At school, we do many different activities.

Every morning, we show respect to the flag.
We stand up and face the flag.
We put our right hand over our heart.
And we say the Pledge of Allegiance.

We learn many subjects at school.
We learn how to read and write.
We learn how to solve math problems.
We read maps and learn about the world we live in.
In art and music classes, we do many fun activities.

We study together and play together with our classmates.
We eat lunch in the cafeteria.
We go to the library to get books.
We play ball on the playground.
We get along with each other.

We get along with each other.

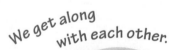

cafeteria

✔ Our Day at School

We learn how to read and write.

We solve math problems.

library

We say the Pledge of Allegiance.

We read maps.

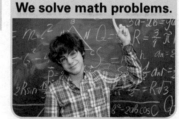

We do fun activities.

playground

Main Idea and Details

1 What is the passage mainly about?

   a. Daily activities at school.   **b.** The Pledge of Allegiance.

   c. The subjects that students learn.   **d.** The friendship among classmates.

2 Where do the students eat lunch?

   a. On the playground.   **b.** In the library.

   c. In the classroom.   **d.** In the cafeteria.

3 What does show respect mean?

   a. Protect.   **b.** Honor.   **c.** Face.   **d.** Listen.

4 Answer the questions.

   a. What do we say in the morning? _____

   b. What do we do in art and music classes? _____

   c. Where do we get books? _____

5 Complete the outline.

Our Day at School

Say the Pledge of Allegiance
- Show respect to the flag
- Stand up, face the ᵃ_____, and put our right hand over our heart

Take classes
- Learn to read, write, and ᵇ_____ math problems
- Learn to read ᶜ_____
- Do fun activities in art and music classes

Do other activities
- Get books from the ᵈ_____
- Eat in the cafeteria
- Play on the playground

Vocabulary Builder

Write the correct word and the meaning in Chinese.

1 ▸ the skills used for painting, sculpting, etc.

_____

2 ▸ an outdoor area where children can play

_____

3 ▸ a student who is in the same class

_____

4 ▸ to have a friendly relationship

_____

Key Words

- rule
- follow
- stay safe
- classroom
- raise
- yell
- hallway
- playground
- obey

We have rules to follow at school.

Rules tell us what to do and what not to do.

Some rules help us get along with one another.

Some rules help us stay safe.

You should follow the rules in your classroom.

Be quiet in the classroom.

Raise your hand before speaking.

You should not yell or run in the classroom.

You should not hit or fight each other.

Do not run in the hallways.

Play ball outside on the playground.

Listen to your teachers and obey them.

Show respect to your teachers.

Teachers teach us and help us follow the rules.

Following the rules makes the school a better place.

✔ Rules We Follow

  Dos

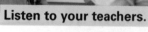
Listen to your teachers.

Raise your hand to talk.

Be quiet in class.

 Don'ts

You should not fight each other.

Do not run in the hallways.

You should not yell in the classroom.

Main Idea and Details

1 **What is the main idea of the passage?**

   a. There are many rules at school.   **b.** Students should always follow the rules.
   c. Teachers make rules for the students.   **d.** It is difficult to follow the rules.

2 **Where should students play ball?**

   a. In the hallways.   **b.** In the classroom.   **c.** On the playground.   **d.** At the gate.

3 **What does follow mean here?**

   a. Obey.   **b.** Remember.   **c.** Make.   **d.** Match.

4 **According to the passage, which statement is true?**

   a. Students should not run on the playground.
   b. Students should not listen to their teachers.
   c. Teachers do not help students follow the rules.
   d. Rules make the school a better place.

5 **Complete the outline.**

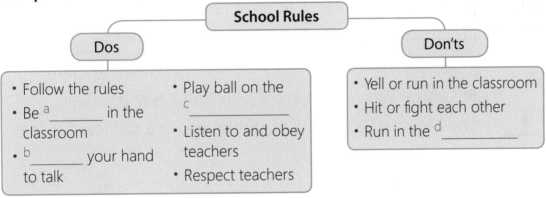

School Rules

Dos

- Follow the rules
- Be ᵃ_____ in the classroom
- ᵇ_____ your hand to talk
- Play ball on the ᶜ_____
- Listen to and obey teachers
- Respect teachers

Don'ts

- Yell or run in the classroom
- Hit or fight each other
- Run in the ᵈ_____

Vocabulary Builder

Write the correct word and the meaning in Chinese.

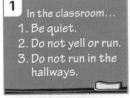   ▸ It tells us what to do and what not to do.

_____

   ▸ to be guided by something

_____

   ▸ to shout loudly; to cry out

_____

   ▸ a narrow passageway in a building

_____

Key Words

- community
- have fun
- neighbor
- neighborhood
- museum
- have a picnic
- police station
- fire station
- service

My name is June.

I live in a community called Chicago.

A community is a place where people live, work, and have fun together.

Chicago is a big city community.

Many people live and work in my community.

My family lives with many neighbors.

Neighbors live close together in a neighborhood.

My home and school are part of my neighborhood.

And my neighborhood is part of my community.

There are many places to have fun in my community.

I can swim in the pool.

I can visit the museum and see many interesting things.

In Central Park, I can have a picnic and play baseball.

The police station and fire station provide services for the community.

My community has many stores for shopping, too.

> I like the neighborhood where I live.

have a picnic

play baseball

swim in the pool

visit the museum

Neighbors live close together.

Main Idea and Details

1 **What is the main idea of the passage?**

a. The people living in communities are neighbors.

b. Communities have many different buildings in them.

c. Our community is where people live, work, and play together.

d. There are many fun places in a community.

2 **What is a neighborhood?**

a. A home and a school.

b. Many places in a community.

c. A place where people live close together.

d. A place with many interesting things.

3 **Which place provides services for a community?**

a. A museum.　　b. A fire station.　　c. A park.　　d. A school.

4 **Complete the sentences.**

a. A city is a large _____.

b. _____ live close to each other in a neighborhood.

c. The _____ _____ and fire station provide services.

5 **Complete the outline.**

My Community

A big city
- A place where people live, work, and have ᵃ_____ together

Neighborhood
- Neighbors live close together
- A ᵇ_____ is part of a community.

Places to have fun
- Can swim in the pool
- Can visit the park and museum
- Can get ᶜ_____ from the fire and police stations
- Can ᵈ_____ at stores

Vocabulary Builder

Write the correct word and the meaning in Chinese.

1 ▸ a place where people live, work, and have fun together

_____

2 ▸ a section of a town or city

_____

3 ▸ a place where important things are kept and displayed

_____

4 ▸ a building for fire equipment and firefighters

_____

Being a Good Citizen

Key Words

- citizen
- member
- state
- respect
- treat
- follow rules
- keep
- help
- care for

Everyone lives in a community.

People in communities need to be good citizens.

A citizen is a member of a community, state, or country.

There are many ways to be a good citizen.

A good citizen respects others.

Treat others as you would like to be treated.

A good citizen follows rules.

We have rules that we must all follow.

Rules keep a community clean and safe.

Another way to be a good citizen is to help others.

Try to be a good neighbor.

Good neighbors help each other and care for one another.

✓ There are many ways to be a good citizen.

respect others

help others

follows rules

care for one another

keep the community clean

14

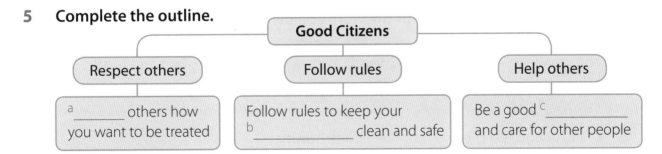

1   **What is the main idea of the passage?**

   a. Everyone is a good citizen.

   b. Good citizens always help others.

   c. People should be good citizens.

   d. Everyone should follow rules.

2   **What does a good citizen do?**

   a. Breaks the rules.   **b.** Respects others.

   c. Has neighbors.   **d.** Keep his or her house clean and safe.

3   **What does treat mean?**

   a. Look toward.   **b.** Show toward.   **c.** Talk toward.   **d.** Act toward.

4   **According to the passage, which statement is true?**

   a. Good citizens are good neighbors.

   b. Good citizens cannot help others.

   c. Good citizens do not need to follow the rules.

   d. Good citizens respect the elders only.

5   **Complete the outline.**

Good Citizens

Respect others	Follow rules	Help others
a _____ others how you want to be treated	Follow rules to keep your b _____ clean and safe	Be a good c _____ and care for other people

Write the correct word and the meaning in Chinese.

 ▸ a member of a community, state, or country

_____

 ▸ a region of a country that has its own government

_____

 ▸ to act or behave toward someone in a certain manner

_____

 ▸ to look after someone or something

_____

Review 1

A Complete the sentences with the words below.

hallways	each other	library	face
stay safe	show respect	quiet	right

1 Every morning, we _____ _____ to the flag.

2 We stand up and _____ the flag.

3 We put our _____ hand over our heart.

4 We get along with _____ _____.

5 We go to the _____ to get books.

6 Some rules help us _____ _____.

7 Be _____ in the classroom.

8 Do not run in the _____.

B Complete the sentences with the words below.

ways	neighborhood	respects	follows
city	police station	care for	shopping

1 Chicago is a big _____ community.

2 Neighbors live close together in a _____.

3 The _____ _____ provides services for the community.

4 My community has many stores for _____.

5 There are many _____ to be a good citizen.

6 A good citizen _____ others.

7 A good citizen _____ rules.

8 Good neighbors _____ _____ one another.

Write the correct word and the meaning in Chinese.

1 ▸ a student who is in the same class

_____

2 ▸ an outdoor area where children can play

_____

3 ▸ a place where people live, work, and have fun together

_____

4 ▸ a person who lives close to another

_____

5 ▸ a member of a community, state, or country

_____

6 ▸ work done by one person or group that benefits another

_____

Match each word with the correct definition and write the meaning in Chinese.

1 activity _____ ☐

2 face _____ ☐

3 get along _____ ☐

4 classroom _____ ☐

5 yell _____ ☐

6 obey _____ ☐

7 museum _____ ☐

8 service _____ ☐

9 respect _____ ☐

10 treat _____ ☐

a. to look at or to look in some direction

b. to have a friendly relationship

c. a room in a school where classes are taught

d. a thing you do at school for an educational experience

e. to treat others in a special way

f. to follow

g. a job that a person does to help others

h. a place where important things are kept and displayed

i. to act or behave toward someone in a certain manner

j. to shout loudly; to cry out

Celebrating Holidays

Key Words

- celebrate
- holiday
- honor
- memorial
- veteran
- independence
- parade
- fireworks
- labor

We celebrate holidays every year.

A holiday is a special day.

Every country has some special days.

In the U.S., people celebrate holidays to honor important people or events.

On national holidays, the whole country celebrates together.

We also fly the flag on these days.

Martin Luther King, Jr. Day is celebrated in January.

Dr. King worked hard for African-Americans.

Memorial Day and Veterans Day honor the people who fought for the country.

Independence Day is celebrated on the 4th of July.

It is the country's birthday.

People celebrate that day with parades and fireworks.

On Labor Day, people show respect for working people.

Independence Day celebration

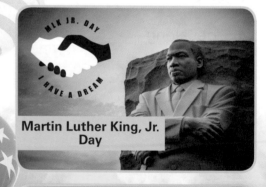

Martin Luther King, Jr. Day

Memorial Day

Veterans Day celebration

Main Idea and Details

1 **What is the main idea of the passage?**

    a. People have parades on some holidays.   **b.** Most holidays honor people.

    c. Every country has some special days.   **d.** There are many kinds of holidays.

2 **There are often fireworks on** _____.

    a. Labor Day   **b.** Memorial Day   **c.** Veterans Day   **d.** Independence Day

3 **What does honor mean here?**

    a. Fight.   **b.** Remember.   **c.** Follow.   **d.** Please.

4 **According to the passage, which statement is true?**

    a. Martin Luther King, Jr. Day is on July 4.

    b. We fly the flag on national holidays.

    c. Memorial Day honors African-Americans.

    d. People celebrate Labor Day with fireworks and parades.

5 **Complete the outline.**

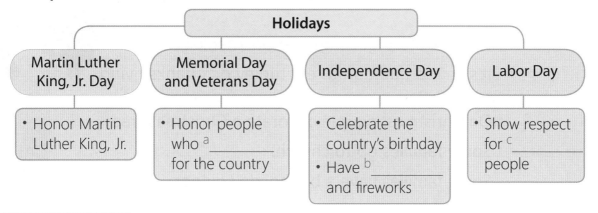

Holidays

Martin Luther King, Jr. Day	Memorial Day and Veterans Day	Independence Day	Labor Day
• Honor Martin Luther King, Jr.	• Honor people who a_____ for the country	• Celebrate the country's birthday • Have b_____ and fireworks	• Show respect for c_____ people

Vocabulary Builder

Write the correct word and the meaning in Chinese.

1 ▸ to do something special for a special occasion

_____

2 ▸ a public celebration with a group of people move through an area

_____

3  ▸ someone who fought in a war as a soldier

_____

4 ▸ getting free from the control of another country

_____

06

Key Words

- tradition
- present (= gift)
- dress up
- costume
- trick-or-treat
- get together
- turkey
- decorate
- go to church

Many holidays have special traditions.
A tradition is a special way that something has been done for a long time. Traditions are repeated year after year.

On Mother's Day, people give presents to their mothers.
On Father's Day, people give presents to their fathers.
Couples give each other gifts on Valentine's Day.

Children dress up in scary costumes on Halloween.
Then they go trick-or-treating for candy.

On Chinese New Year, people usually watch parades.
The dragon parade is a tradition on this holiday.

Families often get together on Thanksgiving.
It's an old tradition to eat turkey on Thanksgiving.

On Christmas, people decorate a Christmas tree.
Some families go to church.
Some families have a big holiday dinner.

The Special Things We Do on Holidays

trick-or-treating
on Halloween

big turkey meal
on Thanksgiving

decorating a Christmas
tree on Christmas

the dragon parade
on Chinese New Year

Main Idea and Details

1 What is the passage mainly about?

a. Different holiday traditions.　　b. The gifts people give on holidays.

c. When each holiday is.　　d. Special holidays around the world.

2 When do children go trick-or-treating?

a. On Christmas.　　b. On Thanksgiving.　　c. On Halloween.　　d. On Father's Day.

3 What does traditions mean?

a. Presents.　　b. Customs.　　c. Costumes.　　d. Parades.

4 Answer the questions.

a. Who gives gifts on Valentine's Day?　　_____

b. What do people do on Chinese New Year?　　_____

c. When do families eat turkey together?　　_____

5 Complete the outline.

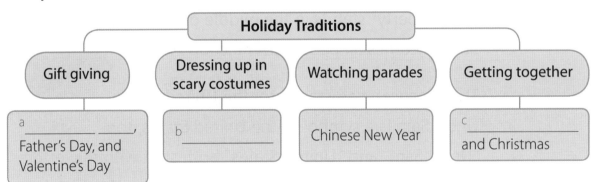

Holiday Traditions

- Gift giving
  - a _____ _____, Father's Day, and Valentine's Day
- Dressing up in scary costumes
  - b _____
- Watching parades
  - Chinese New Year
- Getting together
  - c _____ and Christmas

Vocabulary Builder

Write the correct word and the meaning in Chinese.

1 ▸ to meet in order to spend time together

_____

2 ▸ to make something look prettier

_____

3 ▸ to wear special clothes

_____

4 ▸ to attend church services

_____

America's Symbols

Key Words

- symbol
- stand for (= symbolize)
- freedom
- announce
- symbolize
- statue
- hope
- welcome

Every country has its own symbols.
A symbol is an object that stands for something else.

There are many American symbols.
The Liberty Bell stands for freedom.
The Liberty Bell was rung on July 8, 1776.
It announced America's freedom from England.

The bald eagle is the national bird.
It also symbolizes freedom.

The Statue of Liberty stands for hope and freedom.
"Lady Liberty" stands in the middle of New York Harbor.
She welcomes all people to the country.

The American flag stands for the United States.
Uncle Sam is a symbol of the United States, too.
"Uncle Sam" and "United States" both start with the letters "U.S."
He also wears red, white, and blue clothes like the American flag.

✓ American Symbols

The Liberty Bell

The bald eagle

Uncle Sam

The American flag

The Statue of Liberty

Main Idea and Details

1 **What is the passage mainly about?**

a. The American flag.   b. The Liberty Bell.

c. American symbols.   d. American traditions.

2 **What does the Liberty Bell stand for?**

a. Hope.   b. Freedom.   c. The United States.   d. The American flag.

3 **What does freedom mean?**

a. Hope.   b. Relief.   c. Welcome.   d. Liberty.

4 **Complete the sentences.**

a. The _____ _____ rang to announce America's freedom from England.

b. The Statue of Liberty is also called _____ _____.

c. _____ _____ wears red, white, and blue clothing.

5 **Complete the outline.**

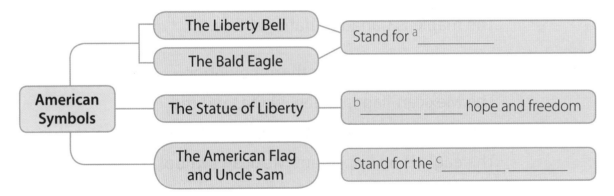

American Symbols

The Liberty Bell
The Bald Eagle
— Stand for ᵃ_____

The Statue of Liberty
— ᵇ_____ _____ hope and freedom

The American Flag and Uncle Sam
— Stand for the ᶜ_____ _____

Vocabulary Builder

Write the correct word and the meaning in Chinese.

1 ► an object that stands for something else

_____

2 ► to be a symbol of something

_____

→ USA

3 ► the feeling of wanting something to happen

_____

4 ► to greet someone who has arrived at a place in a friendly way

_____

National Flags

08

Key Words

- **flag**
- **Stars and Stripes**
- **represent**
- **current**
- **Canadian**
- **maple leaf**
- **eagle**
- **cactus**

Every country has a national flag.

A national flag is a symbol that stands for a country.

The American flag is called the Stars and Stripes.

The flag has 13 stripes and 50 stars.

The 13 stripes represent the first 13 states of the U.S.

The 50 stars represent the current 50 states of the U.S.

The flag's colors are red, white, and blue.

Canada is America's northern neighbor.

The Canadian flag is red and white and has a big maple leaf in the middle.

The maple is Canada's national tree.

Mexico is America's southern neighbor.

The Mexican flag is green, white, and red.

In the center, there is an eagle eating a snake on a cactus.

The eagle is an important Mexican symbol.

✔ National Flags of Many Countries

50 stars

13 stripes

Mexico's flag

maple leaf

golden eagle

America's flag

Canada's flag

Main Idea and Details

1 What is the main idea of the passage?

　a. All flags have symbols on them.

　b. The national flags are usually very colorful.

　c. The U.S., Canada, and Mexico have national flags.

　d. The American flag has 13 stripes and 50 stars.

2 Which symbol is on Mexico's flag?

　a. A maple leaf.　　**b.** A star.　　**c.** An eagle.　　**d.** A circle.

3 What does represent mean?

　a. Show.　　**b.** Stand for.　　**c.** Point.　　**d.** Look up.

4 According to the passage, which statement is true?

　a. The United States' flag is red, white, and blue.

　b. Canada's flag is red and blue.

　c. Mexico's flag is green, blue, and red.

　d. The United States' flag has 13 stars and 50 stripes.

5 Complete the outline.

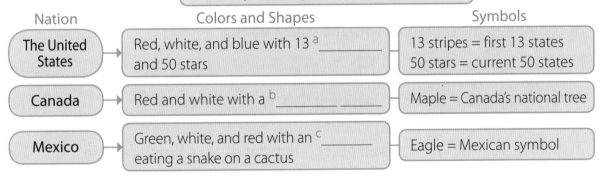

Nation	Colors and Shapes	Symbols
Every Country Has a National Flag		
The United States	Red, white, and blue with 13 ᵃ_____ and 50 stars	13 stripes = first 13 states 50 stars = current 50 states
Canada	Red and white with a ᵇ_____ _____	Maple = Canada's national tree
Mexico	Green, white, and red with an ᶜ_____ eating a snake on a cactus	Eagle = Mexican symbol

Vocabulary Builder

Write the correct word and the meaning in Chinese.

▸ the American flag

_____

▸ relating to Canada

_____

▸ to be a sign or symbol of something

_____

▸ belonging to the present

_____

A

Complete the sentences with the words below.

> national holidays   Thanksgiving   celebrate   costumes
> Mother's Day   Independence   traditions   fly

1   We _____ holidays every year.

2   On _____ _____, the whole country celebrates together.

3   We _____ the flag on national holidays.

4   _____ Day is celebrated on the 4th of July.

5   Many holidays have special _____.

6   On _____ _____, people give presents to their mothers.

7   Children dress up in scary _____ on Halloween.

8   It's an old tradition to eat turkey on _____.

B

Complete the sentences with the words below.

> maple leaf   Liberty Bell   freedom   symbol
> bald eagle   national flag   Mexican   represent

1   A _____ is an object that stands for something else.

2   The _____ _____ stands for freedom. It was rung on July 8, 1776.

3   The _____ _____ is the national bird.

4   The Statue of Liberty stands for hope and _____.

5   A _____ _____ is a symbol that stands for a country.

6   The 50 stars _____ the current 50 states of the U.S.

7   The Canadian flag has a big _____ _____ in the middle.

8   The eagle is an important _____ symbol.

Write the correct word and the meaning in Chinese.

 ▸ to make (something) known in a public

_____

 ▸ a gift

_____

 ▸ to make something look prettier

_____

 ▸ an object that stands for something else

_____

 ▸ to do something special for an important event

_____

 ▸ a large sculpture of a person or an animal

_____

D

Match each word with the correct definition and write the meaning in Chinese.

1 celebrate _____ ☐

2 national holiday _____ ☐

3 independence _____ ☐

4 tradition _____ ☐

5 Mexican _____ ☐

6 dress up _____ ☐

7 scary _____ ☐

8 announce _____ ☐

9 Canadian _____ ☐

10 current _____ ☐

a. frightening
b. relating to Mexico
c. belonging to the present
d. to wear special clothes
e. to tell people about something publicly
f. relating to Canada
g. a special day that the whole country celebrates together
h. getting free from the control of another country
i. to do something special for a special occasion
j. a way that something has been done for a long time

America's Capital

Key Words

- **capital**
- **leader**
- **president**
- **lead**
- **government**
- **governor**
- **state capital**

Washington, D.C. is the capital of the United States.
A capital is the city where many important leaders of a country work.

The president lives and works in the country's capital.
The president leads the country.
He works with other government leaders.

In the U.S., each state has a capital, too.
For example, Phoenix is the capital city of Arizona.
Honolulu is the capital city of Hawaii.

The governor lives and works in the state capital.
The governor is the leader of the state.
Every state has a governor.
The governor works with other state leaders.

✔ Washington, D.C. is the capital of the United States.
✔ In the U.S., each state has a capital, too.

Phoenix
the capital city of Arizona

Honolulu
the capital city of Hawaii

Washington, D.C.

Main Idea and Details

1 What is the main idea of the passage?

a. Every American state has a capital.   **b.** Washington, D.C. is the U.S. capital.

c. Countries and states have capitals.   **d.** A capital is where the governor works.

2 What is the capital of Arizona?

a. Washington, D.C.   **b.** Honolulu.   **c.** Phoenix.   **d.** Hawaii.

3 What does leads mean?

a. Owns.   **b.** Runs.   **c.** Works.   **d.** Lives.

4 Answer the questions.

a. What is a capital? _____

b. Who leads the United States? _____

c. What is a governor? _____

5 Complete the outline.

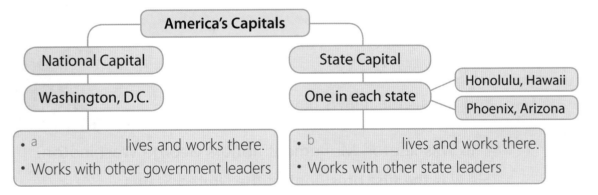

Vocabulary Builder

Write the correct word and the meaning in Chinese.

1 ▸ the city where a country's or state's leaders work

_____

2 ▸ the group of people who run a country or state

_____

3 ▸ the leader of a country

_____

4 ▸ the leader of a state

_____

Key Words

- White House
- Capitol
- capitol
- law
- dome style
- Supreme Court
- judge
- court
- monument

One of the most important cities in the U.S. is Washington, D.C.
Why is it so important?
Because it is the center of the national government.

The White House is in Washington, D.C.
The president of the United States lives and works in the White House. The White House is a symbol of the nation's leader.

The Capitol is there, too.
A capitol is a building where people meet to make laws.
The dome style is also a symbol of the capitol buildings in each state.

The Supreme Court is also there.
Judges work in a court.
Judges decide if laws have been broken.

The Washington Monument honors George Washington.
He was the first president of the United States.

✓ Washington, D.C.

White House

Capitol

Washington Monument

Supreme Court

Main Idea and Details

1 **What is the passage mainly about?**

a. The job that the Supreme Court does. **b.** Where the president works.
c. Why Washington, D.C. is important. **d.** Where people meet to make laws.

2 **Which building has a dome?**

a. The White House. **b.** The Supreme Court.
c. The Washington Monument. **d.** The Capitol.

3 **What does laws mean?**

a. Symbols. **b.** Rules. **c.** Centers. **d.** Courts.

4 **Complete the sentences.**

a. The center of the _____ government is Washington, D.C.

b. People make laws in the _____.

c. _____ work in the Supreme Court.

5 **Complete the outline.**

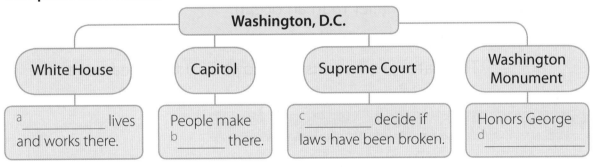

Washington, D.C.

White House	Capitol	Supreme Court	Washington Monument
a _____ lives and works there.	People make b _____ there.	c _____ decide if laws have been broken.	Honors George d _____

Vocabulary Builder

Write the correct word and the meaning in Chinese.

 **1** ▸ a roof shaped like the top half of a ball

_____

 **2** ▸ someone who decides if laws have been broken

_____

 **3** ▸ the building where people make the laws of the country

_____

4 ▸ a building or statue that is built to remember a person or an event

_____

Geography

Our Land and Water

  11

The earth has many different shapes of land.
These different shapes are called landforms.

A mountain is the highest form of land.
A hill is not as high as a mountain.
We call the area between two mountains a valley.
A forest is an area covered with many kinds of trees.
A plain is a large, flat land.

A landform that is surrounded by water is called an island.
An ocean is the largest body of water.
Oceans cover most of the earth's surface.
A lake is smaller than an ocean.
A river is a long body of water.
The water in a river usually flows into the ocean or a lake.

✔ The earth has different landforms and water.

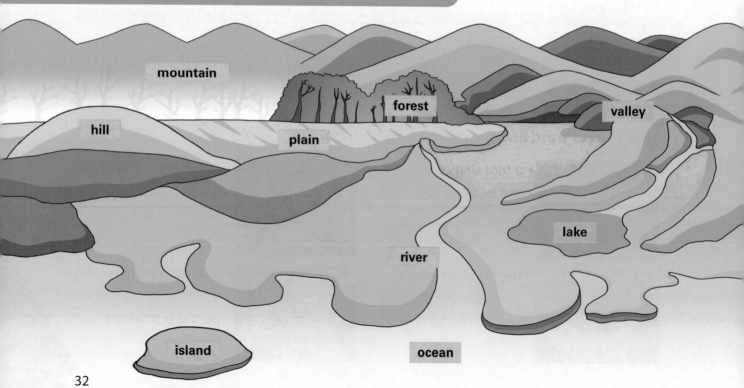

Main Idea and Details

1 **What is the main idea of the passage?**

    a. Water covers most of the earth.

    b. There are many forms of land and water on the earth.

    c. Mountains and hills cover a lot of the earth.

    d. Most of the earth is flat land.

2 **What is the land between two mountains called?**

    a. A plain.   **b.** A forest.   **c.** A valley.   **d.** A hill.

3 **What does flows mean?**

    a. Runs.   **b.** Surrounds.   **c.** Covers.   **d.** Shapes.

4 **According to the passage, which statement is true?**

    a. Oceans are smaller than lakes.   **b.** Mountains are higher than hills.

    c. Oceans flow into rivers or lakes.   **d.** Plains are covered with trees.

5 **Complete the outline.**

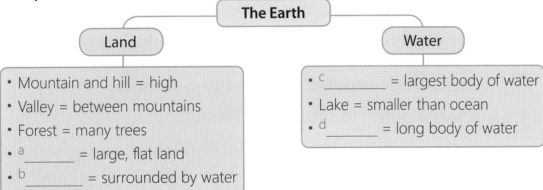

The Earth

Land

- Mountain and hill = high
- Valley = between mountains
- Forest = many trees
- a _____ = large, flat land
- b _____ = surrounded by water

Water

- c _____ = largest body of water
- Lake = smaller than ocean
- d _____ = long body of water

Vocabulary Builder

Write the correct word and the meaning in Chinese.

 **1** ▸ many different shapes of land

_____

 **2** ▸ a large, flat land

_____

 **3** ▸ the area between two mountains

_____

 **4** ▸ an area covered with many kinds of trees

_____

Key Words

- continent
- Old World
- New World
- ocean
- be located in
- next to
- to the east/west of
- map

The world has seven continents.

A continent is a very large piece of land.

Can you name the seven continents?

They are Asia, Africa, Australia, Europe, Antarctica,

and North and South America.

Asia is the largest continent on Earth.

Antarctica is the coldest continent on Earth.

Asia, Africa, and Europe are often called "the Old World."

North and South America are often called "the New World."

The world has five oceans, too.

They are the Pacific, Atlantic, Indian, Antarctic, and Arctic Oceans.

The Pacific is the biggest.

The United States is located in North America.

Canada is next to the U.S. to the north.

Mexico is next to the U.S. to the south.

The Atlantic Ocean is to the east of the U.S.

The Pacific Ocean is to the west of the U.S.

Can you find where your country is on a map?

The world has 7 continents and 5 oceans.

Main Idea and Details

1 **What is the passage mainly about?**

a. The Old World and the New World.

b. The United States.

c. North America.

d. The continents and oceans.

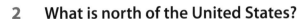

The Pacific Ocean

2 **What is north of the United States?**

a. Mexico.   b. The Pacific Ocean.   c. Canada.   d. Antarctica.

3 **What does piece mean?**

a. Shape.   b. Area.   c. Island.   d. Form.

4 **Answer the questions.**

a. How many continents are there? _____

b. What is the coldest continent? _____

c. What are the five oceans? _____

5 **Complete the outline.**

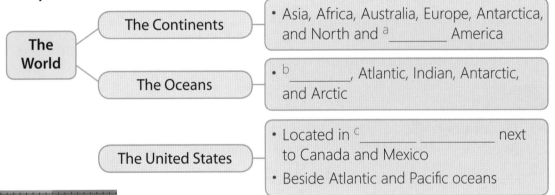

The World

The Continents — • Asia, Africa, Australia, Europe, Antarctica, and North and ª_____ America

The Oceans — • ᵇ_____, Atlantic, Indian, Antarctic, and Arctic

The United States — • Located in ᶜ_____ _____ next to Canada and Mexico
• Beside Atlantic and Pacific oceans

Vocabulary Builder

Write the correct word and the meaning in Chinese.

1 ▸ a very large piece of land

_____

2 ▸ to be situated in; to lie in

_____

3 ▸ the coldest continent on Earth

_____

4 ▸ being close to; beside

_____

Vocabulary ▶ **Review 3**

A Complete the sentences with the words below.

> Washington, D.C.   governor   capitol   honors
> White House   state capital   leads   Court

1 _____ is the capital of the United States.

2 The president _____ the country.

3 The governor lives and works in the _____ _____.

4 The _____ is the leader of the state.

5 The president of the United States lives and works in the _____ _____.

6 A _____ is a building where people meet to make laws.

7 The Supreme _____ is also in Washington, D.C.

8 The Washington Monument _____ George Washington.

B Complete the sentences with the words below.

> Antarctica   flows into   surrounded by   oceans
> continents   next to   located in   valley

1 We call the area between two mountains a _____.

2 A landform that is _____ _____ water is called an island.

3 _____ cover most of the earth's surface.

4 The water in a river usually _____ _____ the ocean or a lake.

5 The world has seven _____.

6 _____ is the coldest continent on Earth.

7 The United States is _____ _____ North America.

8 Canada is _____ _____ the U.S. to the north.

C

Write the correct word and the meaning in Chinese.

1 ▸ the city where a country's or state's leaders work

_____

2 ▸ many different shapes of land

_____

3 ▸ the building where people make the laws of the country

_____

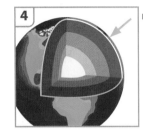

4 ▸ the outside of something

_____

5 ▸ a building or statue that is built to remember a person or an event

_____

6 ▸ a very large piece of land

_____

D

Match each word with the correct definition and write the meaning in Chinese.

1 government _____ ☐

2 governor _____ ☐

3 White House _____ ☐

4 Supreme Court _____ ☐

5 monument _____ ☐

6 landform _____ ☐

7 plain _____ ☐

8 be located in _____ ☐

9 Pacific Ocean _____ ☐

10 Old World _____ ☐

a. the leader of a state

b. a large, flat land

c. to be situated in; to lie in

d. Asia, Africa, and Europe

e. the highest court in a country

f. many different shapes of land

g. the biggest ocean in the world

h. a building or statue that is built to remember a person or an event

i. the group of people who run a country or state

j. the place where the president of the U.S. lives and works

Wrap-Up Test 1

Write the correct word for each sentence.

| citizen | traditions | get along | symbol | covered |
| continents | stands for | national flag | celebrate | oceans |

1   We _____ _____ with each other at school.

2   There are many ways to be a good _____.

3   We _____ holidays every year.

4   Many holidays have special _____.

5   A _____ is an object that stands for something else.

6   The Liberty Bell _____ _____ freedom.

7   A _____ _____ is a symbol that stands for a country.

8   The world has seven _____ and five oceans.

9   _____ cover most of the earth's surface.

10 A forest is an area _____ with many kinds of trees.

B

Write the meanings of the words in Chinese.

1	citizen	_____	16	symbol	_____
2	state	_____	17	stand for	_____
3	care for	_____	18	statue	_____
4	community	_____	19	monument	_____
5	neighbor	_____	20	celebrate	_____
6	rule	_____	21	national holiday	_____
7	respect	_____	22	independence	_____
8	hallway	_____	23	special	_____
9	playground	_____	24	dress up	_____
10	flag	_____	25	current	_____
11	map	_____	26	landform	_____
12	classmate	_____	27	plain	_____
13	follow	_____	28	be located in	_____
14	get along	_____	29	be covered with	_____
15	decorate	_____	30	be surrounded by	_____

2

● Science

Parts of Plants

  13

Key Words

- plant
- root
- absorb
- nutrient
- soil
- hold
- stem
- support
- leaf
- flower
- seed
- grow into

Plants have many parts.

Each part of a plant helps the plant get what it needs.

Roots absorb water and nutrients from the soil.

The roots also hold the plant in the ground.

Stems support the plant's leaves and flowers.

The stems also carry water and nutrients to other plant parts.

Leaves make food for the plant.

Leaves use sunlight and air to make the food.

Most plants also have flowers.

Flowers help plants make new plants.

The flowers make seeds, and then the seeds grow into new plants.

✔ Plants have many parts.

Plants parts can look different, but they do the same job.

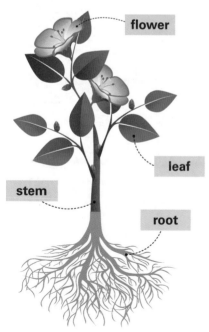

flower

leaf

stem

root

roots

stems

leaves

flowers

Main Idea and Details

1 **What is the main idea of the passage?**

   a. Plants have roots, stems, and leaves.

   b. Plants' parts do many different things.

   c. Without sunlight, plans cannot live.

   d. Most plants have flowers.

seed

2 **What do stems do?**

   a. Hold the plant up.   **b.** Make food for the plant.

   c. Keep the plant in the ground.   **d.** Absorb water from the soil.

3 **What does absorb mean?**

   a. Take over.   **b.** Take in.   **c.** Take out.   **d.** Take off.

4 **Complete the sentences.**

   a. Roots absorb nutrients from the _____.

   b. _____ make the plant's food.

   c. _____ can become new plants.

5 **Complete the outline.**

Parts of Plants

Roots	Stems	Leaves	Flowers
Absorb ᵃ_____ and nutrients from the soil	Carry water and ᵇ_____ to other plant parts	Make ᶜ_____ for the plant	Make ᵈ_____ that grow into new plants

Vocabulary Builder

Write the correct word and the meaning in Chinese.

▸ the part of a plant that grows under the ground

_____

▸ the small, hard part of a plant that can grow into a new plant

_____

▸ the top part of the earth in which plants grow

_____

▸ to become (something) as time passes

_____

What Do Plants Need?

Key Words

- grow
- water
- nutrient
- contain
- air
- sunlight
- take in
- space
- healthy

Have you ever tried to grow a plant?
You probably realized that plants need many things to grow.

First, plants need water.
Plants can get water from the ground or from the rain.
Without water, plants will die.

Plants also need nutrients from the soil.
The soil contains many important nutrients that plants need to grow.

Plants need air and sunlight as well.
Leaves help the plant get the air it needs.
The leaves also take in sunlight to make food for the plant.

Finally, plants need space to grow and to stay healthy.
As plants get bigger, they need more room to grow bigger.

✔ How do plants grow?

Plants need water and nutrients from the soil.

Plants need air and sunlight.

Leaves help the plant get the air it needs.

Plants need space to grow.

Main Idea and Details

1   What is the passage mainly about?

a. How much space plants need.

b. Where to grow plants.

c. What plants need to grow.

d. How leaves make food for the plant.

grow plants

2   What do leaves need to make food?

a. Sunlight.   b. Rain.   c. Seeds.   d. Space.

3   What does contains mean?

a. Makes.   b. Needs.   c. Wants.   d. Holds.

4   Answer the questions.

a. Where can plants get water?   _____

b. Where are there many nutrients?   _____

c. What do plants need to grow bigger?   _____

5   Complete the outline.

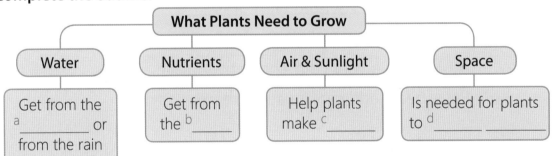

What Plants Need to Grow

Water	Nutrients	Air & Sunlight	Space
Get from the ᵃ_____ or from the rain	Get from the ᵇ_____	Help plants make ᶜ_____	Is needed for plants to ᵈ_____ _____

Vocabulary Builder

Write the correct word and the meaning in Chinese.

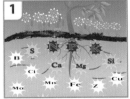
▸ to have (something) inside

_____

▸ to absorb

_____

▸ the mixture of gases that people and animals breathe

_____

▸ physically strong

_____

Key Words

- habitat
- stay safe
- forest
- rainforest
- desert
- grassland
- tundra
- caribou

Do you think polar bears could live in a desert?
How about fish?

Animals live in different places.
The place where an animal lives is its habitat.
Animals can have food and stay safe in their habitat.

A forest habitat has many trees.
Animals like deer, squirrels, and rabbits live there.
A rainforest gets rain almost every day and is hot all year.
Snakes, lizards, and crocodiles live there.
A desert is very dry and has lots of sand.
Small animals, like rats, scorpions, and spiders, live there.
A grassland is covered with grass.
Zebras, giraffes, and elephants live there.
A tundra is a very cold and snowy place.
Polar bears and caribous live there.

✔ Animals and Habitats

deer and squirrels in a forest

zebras and giraffes in a grassland

polar bears and caribous in a tundra

scorpions and spiders in a desert

crocodiles and lizards in a rainforest

Main Idea and Details

1 **What is the passage mainly about?**

　　a. The smallest and largest animals.　　**b.** Habitats where people live.

　　c. Some habitats on the earth.　　**d.** Home of polar bears.

2 **Where do giraffes often live?**

　　a. Rainforests.　　**b.** Grasslands.　　**c.** Forests.　　**d.** Deserts.

3 **What does habitat mean?**

　　a. A place that has food.　　**b.** Forest and desert.

　　c. A place where animals live.　　**d.** A place that rains a lot.

4 **According to the passage, which statement is true?**

　　a. Elephants live in the desert.　　**b.** A tundra has cold weather.

　　c. There are many trees in grasslands.　　**d.** A forest is covered with sand.

5 **Complete the outline.**

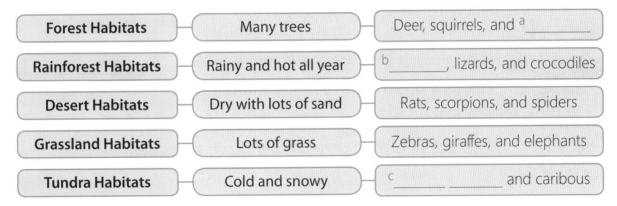

Forest Habitats	Many trees	Deer, squirrels, and ᵃ_____
Rainforest Habitats	Rainy and hot all year	ᵇ_____, lizards, and crocodiles
Desert Habitats	Dry with lots of sand	Rats, scorpions, and spiders
Grassland Habitats	Lots of grass	Zebras, giraffes, and elephants
Tundra Habitats	Cold and snowy	ᶜ_____ _____ and caribous

Vocabulary Builder

Write the correct word and the meaning in Chinese.

1 ▸ a place where plants and animals live

_____

2 ▸ a large type of deer that lives in northern parts of the world

_____

3 ▸ a place covered with grass

_____

4 ▸ a very cold and snowy place

_____

Key Words

- ocean
- salt water
- undersea
- plankton
- fresh water
- breathe
- lungs
- gills
- oxygen

Water covers most of the earth.

So there are many water habitats.

These include ponds, lakes, rivers, and oceans.

Oceans are the earth's biggest habitats.

An ocean is a very large body of salt water.

There is a lot of undersea life in the oceans.

Some animals, like plankton, are so tiny that you can barely see them.

Others, such as whales, are the largest animals on the earth.

Ponds, lakes, and rivers have fresh water.

Many fish live in fresh water, too.

How do fish breathe in the water?

Animals on land have lungs to breathe air.

But fish have gills.

Fish use gills to take in oxygen from the water.

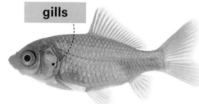

gills

Fish breathe in the water by using gills.

✔ *Oceans are the earth's biggest habitats.*

whale

dolphin

fish

sea turtle

plankton

coral reef

pond

1   What is the main idea of the passage?

a. Whales and plankton live in the ocean.

b. Water habitats have many animals.

c. Fish are able to breathe underwater.

d. Oceans are the earth's biggest habitats.

2   What do fish use to breathe in the water?

a. Plankton.   b. Lungs.   c. Oxygen.   d. Gills.

3   What does life mean?

a. Plants.   b. Rocks.   c. Animals and plants.   d. Tiny fish.

4   Complete the sentences.

a. Most of the earth is covered with _____.

b. _____ have salt water.

c. Ponds, lakes, and rivers have _____ _____.

d. _____ are the largest animals on the earth.

5   Complete the outline.

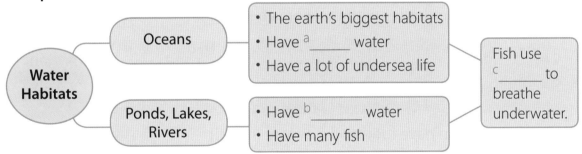

Water Habitats

Oceans
- The earth's biggest habitats
- Have ᵃ_____ water
- Have a lot of undersea life

Ponds, Lakes, Rivers
- Have ᵇ_____ water
- Have many fish

Fish use ᶜ_____ to breathe underwater.

Write the correct word and the meaning in Chinese.

1 ▶ plants and animals under the sea

_____

2 ▶ the largest animal on the earth

_____

3 ▶ very small animals and plants that live in water

_____

4 ▶ the part of a fish that takes in oxygen from the water

_____

A

Complete the sentences with the words below.

| leaves | nutrients | grow | contains |
| support | ground | absorb | sunlight |

1   Roots _____ water and nutrients from the soil.

2   Stems _____ the plant's leaves and flowers.

3   _____ make food for the plant.

4   The flowers make seeds, and then the seeds _____ into new plants.

5   The soil _____ many important nutrients that plants need to grow.

6   Plants can get water from the _____ or from the rain.

7   Plants also need _____ from the soil.

8   Plants need air and _____ as well.

B

Complete the sentences with the words below.

| forest | covered | desert | oxygen |
| habitat | fresh water | whales | oceans |

1   Animals can have food and stay safe in their _____.

2   A _____ habitat has many trees.

3   Small animals, like rats, scorpions, and spiders, live in a _____.

4   A grassland is _____ with grass.

5   _____ are the earth's biggest habitats.

6   _____ are the largest animals on the earth.

7   Many fish live in the _____ _____, too.

8   Fish use gills to take in _____ from the water.

Write the correct word and the meaning in Chinese.

1 ▸ a part of plants that absorbs water and nutrients from the soil

_____

2 ▸ a part of plants that supports the plants' leaves and flowers

_____

3 ▸ to become larger or taller

_____

4 ▸ a rainy and hot place all year long

_____

5 ▸ a very cold and snowy place

_____

6 ▸ plants and animals under the sea

_____

D

Match each word with the correct definition and write the meaning in Chinese.

1 nutrient _____ ☐

2 seed _____ ☐

3 soil _____ ☐

4 hold _____ ☐

5 grow _____ ☐

6 take in _____ ☐

7 healthy _____ ☐

8 desert _____ ☐

9 lungs _____ ☐

10 salt water _____ ☐

a. to get bigger

b. physically strong

c. the body parts used to breathe air

d. to keep; to support

e. seawater; the salty water of the sea

f. to absorb

g. food that helps plants live and grow

h. a very dry place with lots of sand

i. the top part of the earth in which plants grow

j. the small, hard part of a plant that can grow into a new plant

Key Words

- weather
- daily life
- measure
- thermometer
- temperature
- degree
- weather vane
- indicate
- rain gauge

Every day, when people wake up, they look outside.

What are they doing?

They are checking the weather.

Weather affects our daily lives a lot.

What is weather?

Weather is what the air outside is like.

The weather can be sunny, cloudy, rainy, or snowy.

It can change in a few hours or day to day.

How can you measure weather?

We use some tools to measure the weather.

A thermometer measures temperature.

Temperature shows how warm or cold the air is.

We measure the temperature in units called degrees.

Some tools measure wind or rain.

A weather vane indicates the direction of the wind.

A rain gauge is used to find out how much rain falls.

✔ Measuring Tools

The arrow indicates the direction the wind is coming from.

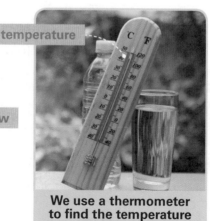

We use a thermometer to find the temperature outside.

A rain gauge measures how much rain falls.

snowy   cloudy

1 What is the passage mainly about?

  a. All kinds of weather.

  b. Weather and how to measure it.

  c. The way to use a thermometer.

  d. How weather affects our daily lives.

2 A _____ measures the amount of rain falling.

  a. Weather vane.   **b.** Thermometer.   **c.** Rain gauge.   **d.** Degree.

3 What does tools mean?

  a. Equipment.   **b.** People.   **c.** Hand.   **d.** Unit.

4 Answer the questions

  a. What are some kinds of weather? _____

  b. What unit do we use to measure the temperature? _____

  c. What does a weather vane measure? _____

5 Complete the outline.

Kinds of Weather — Sunny, cloudy, rainy, and snowy

Weather

Thermometer — Measures ᵃ_____

Weather vane — Measures wind ᵇ_____

Weather Tools

Rain gauge — Measures the amount of ᶜ_____

Write the correct word and the meaning in Chinese.

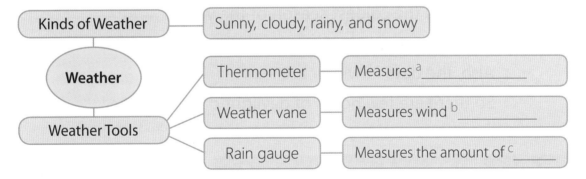

1 ▸ a tool that measures temperature

_____

2 ▸ a tool that measures the direction of the wind; a wind vane

_____

3 ▸ to find out the size, length, or amount of something

_____

4 ▸ a measurement of how hot or cold a place or object is

_____

Key Words

- season
- spring
- summer
- fall
- winter
- get warmer
- day
- hour
- get cooler
- fall off
- daylight

In many places, the weather changes with each season.

There are four seasons: spring, summer, fall, and winter.

In spring, the weather gets warmer.

Most plants begin to grow.

In some places, it rains a lot during spring.

In summer, the weather is usually very hot.

It is the warmest season of the year.

The days in summer are long, so there are many hours of sunlight.

When fall comes, the weather gets cooler.

The leaves change colors and fall off the trees.

Winter is the coldest season of the year.

In some places, it snows a lot during winter.

Also, the days in winter are short.

So there are few hours of daylight during winter.

✔ **How does the weather change in each season?**

spring

gets warmer

summer

very hot

fall

gets cooler

winter

very cold

Main Idea and Details

1   What is the main idea of the passage?

    a. The weather gets warmer in spring.   **b.** Winter is the coldest season.

    c. Most people like the summer.   **d.** All four seasons are different.

2   What do plants do in spring?

    a. They change colors.   **b.** They start growing.   **c.** They die.   **d.** They get stronger.

3   What does days mean here?

    a. A day, 24 hours.   **b.** The time between sunlight and sunset.

    c. Every day.   **d.** Working hours.

4   According to the passage, which statement is true?

    a. Summer comes before spring.   **b.** The days in winter are long.

    c. It rains a lot during summer.   **d.** The leaves change colors in fall.

5   Complete the outline.

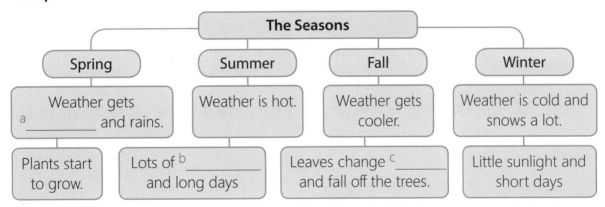

The Seasons

Spring	Summer	Fall	Winter
Weather gets a _____ and rains.	Weather is hot.	Weather gets cooler.	Weather is cold and snows a lot.
Plants start to grow.	Lots of b _____ and long days	Leaves change c _____ and fall off the trees.	Little sunlight and short days

Vocabulary Builder

Write the correct word and the meaning in Chinese.

1 ▸ one of the four periods into which the year is divided

_____

2 ▸ the period of time when it is light outside

_____

3 ▸ sunlight

_____

4 ▸ to drop down; to come off

_____

What Can You See in the Sky?

Key Words

- clear
- look up
- object
- moon
- move around
- tiny
- star
- far away
- bright
- sun

On a clear night, go outside and look up in the sky.
You can probably see many objects.

The biggest object in the night sky is the moon.
The moon is a huge ball of rock that moves around Earth.

You can see hundreds of tiny stars also.
Actually, a star is a huge ball of hot gases.
Stars look tiny because they are so far away from Earth.
Most stars can be seen only at night.
In the daytime, the sunlight is so bright that you cannot see them.
But they are still there.

During the day, you will see the sun.
Do you know that the sun is a star?
It looks so bright and big because it is the closest star to Earth.

✔ **What can you see in the sky?**

The moon is a huge ball of rock
that moves around Earth.

Stars are always in the sky
even during the daytime.

The sun is the closest
star to Earth.

Main Idea and Details

1 **What is the main idea of the passage?**

   a. Objects in the night sky.   **b.** The sun and the moon.

   c. The stars in the sky.   **d.** The biggest object in the sky.

2 **What can you see only at night?**

   a. The sun.   **b.** The stars.   **c.** The moon.   **d.** The sky.

3 **What does moves around mean?**

   a. Goes around.   **b.** Goes down.   **c.** Comes up.   **d.** Comes across.

4 **Complete the sentences.**

   a. The _____ is a huge ball of rock.

   b. Stars look _____ because they are so far away from Earth.

   c. The _____ is the closest star to Earth.

5 **Complete the outline.**

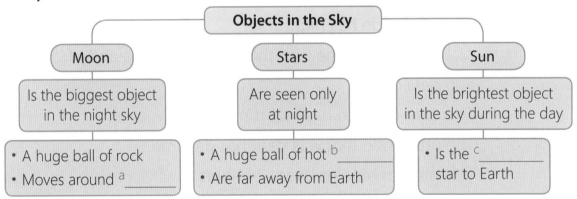

Objects in the Sky

Moon	Stars	Sun
Is the biggest object in the night sky	Are seen only at night	Is the brightest object in the sky during the day
• A huge ball of rock • Moves around ᵃ_____	• A huge ball of hot ᵇ_____ • Are far away from Earth	• Is the ᶜ_____ star to Earth

Vocabulary Builder

Write the correct word and the meaning in Chinese.

 ▸ to raise your eyes

_____

 ▸ full of light

_____

 ▸ very small

_____

 ▸ a long distance from

_____

What Causes Day and Night?

20

Key Words

- rise
- set
- rotate
  (= spin around)
- rotation
- cause
- shape
- daytime
- nighttime
- repeat

Each day, the sun seems to rise in the morning and set at night. But the sun is not really moving. Earth is moving.

Earth rotates.

To rotate means to spin around like a top.

It takes 24 hours for Earth to rotate one time.

One rotation is one day.

Earth's rotation causes day and night.

Earth is shaped like a ball.

As Earth rotates, there is sunlight where Earth faces the sun.

That part of Earth has daytime.

The other side has nighttime.

As Earth rotates, the part that was light turns away from the sun and gets dark.

That part of Earth has nighttime.

The other side that was dark has daytime.

This pattern repeats every 24 hours.

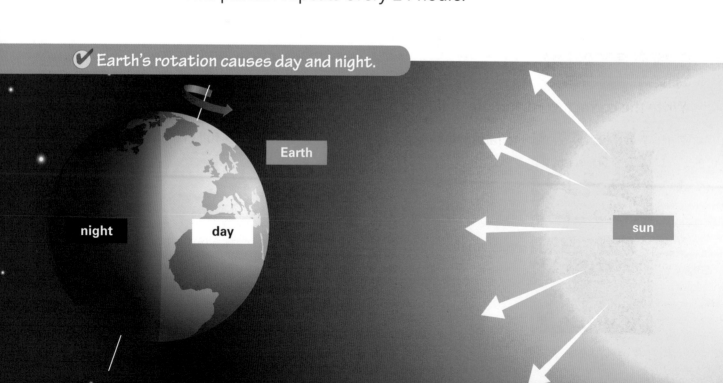

✓ Earth's rotation causes day and night.

night   day   Earth   sun

Main Idea and Details

1 **What is the passage mainly about?**

   a. Where day and night are happening.   **b.** How long day and night last.

   c. Why we have day and night.   **d.** What if there are no day and night.

2 **What does Earth do in 24 hours?**

   a. It makes a complete rotation.   **b.** It orbits the sun.

   c. It finishes an entire night.   **d.** It changes from day to night many times.

3 **What does rotates mean?**

   a. Goes around.   **b.** Looks around.   **c.** Moves around.   **d.** Spins around.

4 **Answer the questions.**

   a. What is Earth's shape? _____

   b. How long is one day? _____

   c. When a side of Earth faces away from the sun, what time of day is it? _____

5 **Complete the outline.**

> **Earth's Rotation Causes Day and Night**

| It takes 24 hours for Earth to rotate once. | → | One day |

| The part where Earth faces the sun | → | a _____ |

| The part where Earth is turned ᵇ_____ from the sun | → | Nighttime |

Vocabulary Builder

Write the correct word and the meaning in Chinese.

 ▸ to go down

_____

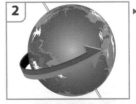 ▸ to turn; to spin around

_____

 ▸ to give a particular form to something

_____

 ▸ the period of time when it is dark

_____

A Complete the sentences with the words below.

degrees	season	measure	rain
cloudy	fall off	warmest	daylight

1 The weather can be sunny, _____, rainy, or snowy.

2 How can you _____ weather?

3 We measure the temperature in units called _____.

4 A rain gauge is used to find out how much _____ falls.

5 In many places, the weather changes with each _____.

6 Summer is the _____ season of the year.

7 The leaves change colors and _____ _____ the trees in fall.

8 There are few hours of _____ during winter.

B Complete the sentences with the words below.

gases	far away	moon	causes
rotates	rotation	bright	takes

1 The biggest object in the night sky is the _____.

2 Actually, a star is a huge ball of hot _____.

3 Stars look tiny because they are so _____ _____ from Earth.

4 In the daytime, the sunlight is so _____ that you cannot see stars.

5 It _____ 24 hours for Earth to rotate one time.

6 One _____ of Earth is one day.

7 Earth's rotation _____ day and night.

8 As Earth _____, there is sunlight where Earth faces the sun.

C

Write the correct word and the meaning in Chinese.

1 ▸ a tool that measures temperature

_____

2 ▸ sunlight

_____

3 ▸ a tool that measures the amount of rain

_____

4 ▸ very small

_____

5 ▸ to go down

_____

6 ▸ to turn; to spin around

_____

D

Match each word with the correct definition and write the meaning in Chinese.

1 indicate _____ ☐

2 get warmer _____ ☐

3 get cooler _____ ☐

4 daylight _____ ☐

5 fall off _____ ☐

6 look up _____ ☐

7 object _____ ☐

8 far away _____ ☐

9 cause _____ ☐

10 repeat _____ ☐

a. sunlight

b. to show

c. a long distance from

d. to make something happen

e. to become colder

f. to become hotter

g. to drop down; to come off

h. to raise your eyes

i. to do something again and again

j. a thing you can see, hold, or touch

Solids, Liquids, and Gases

Key Words

- **be made of**
- **matter**
- **solid**
- **liquid**
- **gas**
- **hard**
- **container**
- **fill**

Everything in the world is made of matter.

Air, water, and this book are all made of matter.

Matter has three forms.

They are solids, liquids, and gases.

A solid is a hard object that can be touched.

Only a solid has a shape of its own.

Cars, books, rocks, and ice are all solids.

Water is a liquid.

A liquid does not have a shape of its own.

It takes the shape of its container.

Juice, milk, and coke are all liquids.

Air is made up of gases.

Like a liquid, a gas does not have its own shape.

It fills all of the space of its container.

The air inside balloons, helium, and steam is all gases.

What are solids?

What are liquids?

What are gases?

Main Idea and Details

1 What is the passage mainly about?

a. Solids and liquids.   b. The three types of matter.

c. Different types of gases.   d. Common hard objects.

2 What are things made of?

a. Solids.   b. Liquids.   c. Matter.   d. Gases.

3 What does forms mean here?

a. Solids.   b. Types.   c. Objects.   d. Shapes.

4 According to the passage, which statement is true?

a. Solid objects have their own shapes.

b. Two liquids are milk and ice.

c. Gases can be solid objects.

d. Air is made up of liquids.

5 Complete the outline.

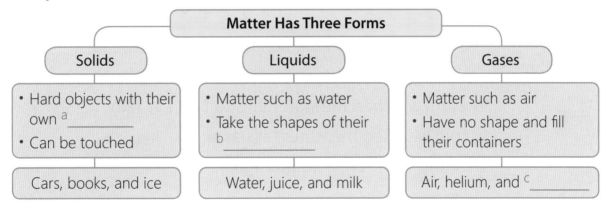

Matter Has Three Forms		
Solids	**Liquids**	**Gases**
• Hard objects with their own ᵃ_____ • Can be touched	• Matter such as water • Take the shapes of their ᵇ_____	• Matter such as air • Have no shape and fill their containers
Cars, books, and ice	Water, juice, and milk	Air, helium, and ᶜ_____

Vocabulary Builder

Write the correct word and the meaning in Chinese.

 ▸ to consist of

_____

 ▸ a hard object that can be touched

_____

 ▸ to make (something) full

_____

 ▸ a form of matter (such as helium) that is like air and has no fixed shape

_____

Key Words

- water vapor
- turn back
- freeze
- water cycle
- turn into
- gather
- in the form of
- release

Water can be a solid, a liquid, or a gas.

When water gets warm, it changes into a gas.

The gas is called water vapor.

When water vapor gets cool, it turns back into water.

Water can change into a solid ice when it freezes.

This water cycle makes it rain or snow.

The sun heats the water in the oceans and on land.

Some water turns into water vapor.

As the water vapor rises into the air,

the temperature gets colder.

This makes the water vapor turn back into water.

The water gathers in the sky in the form of clouds.

Eventually, the clouds release their water.

In warm weather, the water falls to Earth as rain.

In cold weather, the water falls as snow.

Then the water cycle begins again.

✔ Forms of Water

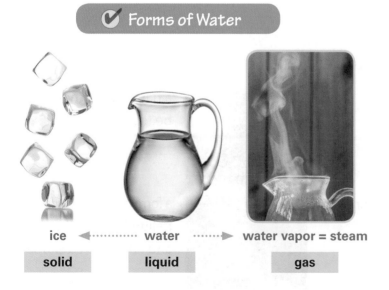

ice ◄······· water ·······► water vapor = steam

solid — **liquid** — **gas**

✔ The Water Cycle

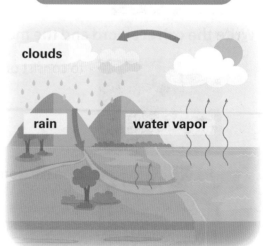

clouds

rain — water vapor

Main Idea and Details

1 What is the passage mainly about?

   a. Water vapor.   **b.** The sun's heat.

   c. The water cycle.   **d.** Forms of water.

2 What makes water change into water vapor?

   a. Hot temperatures.   **b.** Cold temperatures.   **c.** Gas.   **d.** Solid ice.

3 What does water vapor mean?

   a. Ice.   **b.** Water.   **c.** Cloud.   **d.** Steam.

4 Complete the sentences.

   a. Water in its gas form is called _____ _____.

   b. Cold air turns water vapor into _____.

   c. Water falls to the ground as _____ in cold weather.

5 Complete the outline.

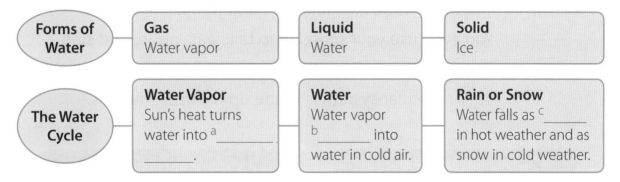

Forms of Water	**Gas** Water vapor	**Liquid** Water	**Solid** Ice
The Water Cycle	**Water Vapor** Sun's heat turns water into ᵃ_____ _____.	**Water** Water vapor ᵇ_____ into water in cold air.	**Rain or Snow** Water falls as ᶜ_____ in hot weather and as snow in cold weather.

Vocabulary Builder

Write the correct word and the meaning in Chinese.

 ▸ steam

_____

 ▸ the circulation of the earth's water

_____

 ▸ to become ice because of cold

_____

 ▸ to let go; to stop holding something

_____

23

Your body has many different parts.

All your parts work together to help you live.

Let's learn about some of the systems of your body.

Bones are the hard body parts inside your body.

They connect each body part to one another.

They hold your body up and give the body its shape.

Bones also protect many important parts inside your body.

There are more than 200 bones inside you.

All together, they form your skeletal system.

Muscles are body parts that make you move.

You use muscles to walk, run, and jump.

You even use your muscles to talk, eat, laugh, and sing.

There are more than 600 muscles inside you.

Your muscular system is made up of these muscles.

Key Words

- bone
- connect
- hold up
- protect
- skeletal system
- muscle
- move
- muscular system

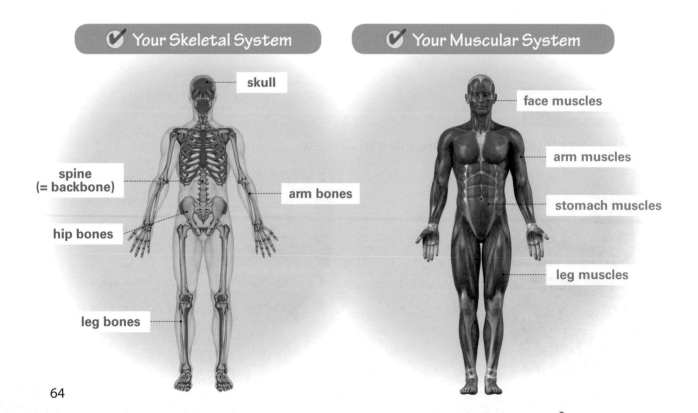

✔ Your Skeletal System

✔ Your Muscular System

skull

spine
(= backbone)

arm bones

hip bones

leg bones

face muscles

arm muscles

stomach muscles

leg muscles

Main Idea and Details

1 What is the main idea of the passage?

a. A body has 200 bones and 600 muscles.

b. Bones and muscles are important to the body.

c. You need bones more than you need muscles.

d. A body has many different parts.

2 What do bones do?

a. Let people run.   b. Protect some body parts.

c. Make the body move.   d. Let people sing.

3 What does connect mean?

a. Work.   b. Move.   c. Join.   d. Hold.

4 Answer the questions.

a. How many bones are in the body? _____

b. How many muscles are in the body? _____

c. What do all of the muscles together make? _____

5 Complete the outline.

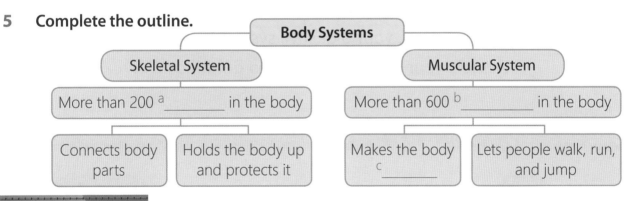

Body Systems

Skeletal System

Muscular System

More than 200 ᵃ_____ in the body

More than 600 ᵇ_____ in the body

Connects body parts

Holds the body up and protects it

Makes the body ᶜ_____

Lets people walk, run, and jump

Vocabulary Builder

Write the correct word and the meaning in Chinese.

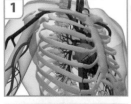

▶ to prevent something from being harmed

_____

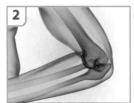

▶ to join two things together

_____

▶ a body part that makes you move

_____

▶ to move your body off the ground using your legs

_____

The Systems of Your Body

Let's learn more about the systems of your body.

Key Words
- breathe
- respiratory
- circulate
- circulatory
- blood vessel
- pump
- carry
- digestive
- break down

You breathe using your respiratory system.
Your mouth and nose take in oxygen from the air.
Then, the oxygen goes into your lungs and moves through your blood.

Blood circulates in your body through your circulatory system.
It is made up of your heart and blood vessels.
Your heart pumps blood through blood vessels.
Blood vessels are small tubes.
They carry blood from your heart to every part of your body.

Your body gets energy from the food you eat.
When you eat, your digestive system breaks down the food.
This lets your body get energy to do things.

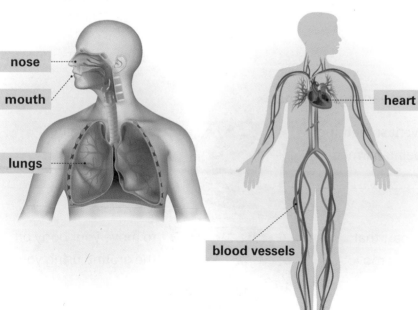

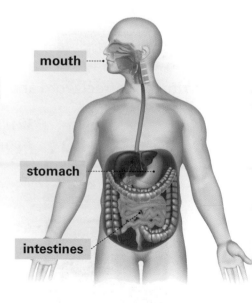

Main Idea and Details

1   **What is the passage mainly about?**

   a. The circulatory system.   **b.** How blood moves in the body.

   c. Some of the body's systems.   **d.** How the body gets energy.

2   **What does the digestive system do?**

   a. It moves blood.   **b.** It breaks down food.

   c. It takes in oxygen.   **d.** It protects the heart.

3   **What does carry mean?**

   a. Take.   **b.** Breathe.   **c.** Eat.   **d.** Use.

4   **According to the passage, which statement is true?**

   a. The lungs are part of the circulatory system.

   b. Blood moves through the body in blood vessels.

   c. The digestive system takes air to the heart.

   d. Blood vessels help break down the food.

5   **Complete the outline.**

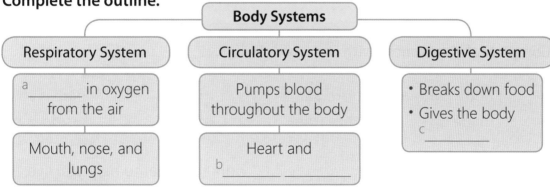

Body Systems

Respiratory System | Circulatory System | Digestive System

a _____ in oxygen from the air | Pumps blood throughout the body | • Breaks down food • Gives the body c _____

Mouth, nose, and lungs | Heart and b _____ _____

Vocabulary Builder

Write the correct word and the meaning in Chinese.

1
▸ to move (blood) through your body by beating

_____

2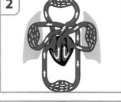
▸ to move around within a system

_____

3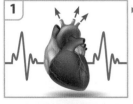
▸ a small tube that carries blood

_____

4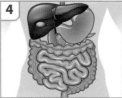
▸ a body system that breaks down the food

_____

A Complete the sentences with the words below.

> water cycle   shape   rain   clouds
> solid   changes   matter   gases

1 Everything in the world is made of _____.

2 A _____ is a hard object that can be touched.

3 A liquid does not have a _____ of its own.

4 The air inside balloons, helium, and steam is all _____.

5 When water gets warm, it _____ into a gas.

6 The _____ _____ makes it rain or snow.

7 The water gathers in the sky in the form of _____.

8 In warm weather, the water falls to Earth as _____.

B Complete the sentences with the words below.

> body parts   circulates   muscles   digestive
> made up   breathe   connect   inside

1 All your _____ _____ work together to help you live.

2 Bones _____ each body part to one another.

3 _____ are body parts that make you move.

4 There are more than 600 muscles _____ you.

5 You _____ using your respiratory system.

6 Blood _____ in your body through your circulatory system.

7 Your circulatory system is _____ _____ of your heart and blood vessels.

8 When you eat, your _____ system breaks down the food.

C

Write the correct word and the meaning in Chinese.

1  ▸ matter such as water

_____

2  ▸ something such as a box, a bowl, or a bottle

_____

3 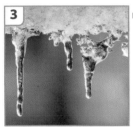 ▸ to become ice because of cold

_____

4 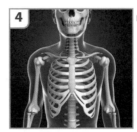 ▸ a body system relating to the bones

_____

5 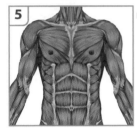 ▸ a body system relating to the muscles

_____

6 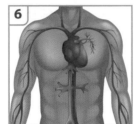 ▸ a body system relating to blood circulation

_____

D

Match each word with the correct definition and write the meaning in Chinese.

1 be made of _____ ☐

2 solid _____ ☐

3 turn back _____ ☐

4 turn into _____ ☐

5 release _____ ☐

6 protect _____ ☐

7 muscle _____ ☐

8 breathe _____ ☐

9 circulate _____ ☐

10 blood vessel _____ ☐

a. to consist of

b. to change into

c. a hard object that can be touched

d. to move around within a system

e. to let go; to stop holding something

f. to go back to one's original state

g. a body part that makes you move

h. a small tube that carries blood

i. to prevent something from being harmed

j. to take air into your lungs and to send it out again

Wrap-Up Test **2**

A

Write the correct word for each sentence.

| carry | matter | respiratory | habitat | rotation |
| season | absorb | water cycle | muscular | weather |

1 Roots _____ water and nutrients from the soil.

2 Stems _____ water and nutrients to other plant parts.

3 Animals can have food and stay safe in their _____.

4 The _____ can be sunny, cloudy, rainy, or snowy.

5 In many places, the weather changes with each _____.

6 Earth's _____ causes day and night.

7 Everything in the world is made of _____.

8 The _____ _____ makes it rain or snow.

9 Your _____ system is made up of muscles.

10 You breathe using your _____ system.

B

Write the meanings of the words in Chinese.

1	root	_____	16	move around	_____
2	stem	_____	17	rotate	_____
3	leaf	_____	18	solid	_____
4	seed	_____	19	liquid	_____
5	nutrient	_____	20	water vapor	_____
6	soil	_____	21	skeletal system	_____
7	hold	_____	22	muscular system	_____
8	grow	_____	23	circulatory system	_____
9	habitat	_____	24	respiratory system	_____
10	tundra	_____	25	digestive system	_____
11	undersea life	_____	26	be made of	_____
12	gill	_____	27	turn into	_____
13	rainforest	_____	28	release	_____
14	salt water	_____	29	breathe	_____
15	thermometer	_____	30	circulate	_____

3

- **Mathematics**
- **Language**
- **Visual Arts**
- **Music**

Shapes and Figures

Key Words

- **shape**
- **triangle**
- **rectangle**
- **side**
- **flat shape**
  (= plane figure)
- **figure**
- **solid shape**
  (= solid figure)
- **sphere**

Can you name these shapes?

A shape with three sides is called a triangle.

A rectangle has four sides.

A square has four sides of equal length.

A circle is round and has no sides.

These shapes are called flat shapes or plane figures.

A figure is a regular shape.

There are many solid shapes, too.

A sphere is a solid-shaped circle.

A cube is a solid-shaped square.

Cones, pyramids, and cylinders are also solid shapes.

Everywhere you look, you can see solid shapes and figures.

They are in buildings and in everyday objects.

Look around your home or school for example.

What figures do you see?

These are flat shapes or plane figures.

side

triangle   rectangle   square   circle   oval

✔ **Solid shapes and figures are in everyday objects. What do they look like?**

 sphere   cube   cylinder   cone   pyramid

globe
ball
ice   dice
soda can   thermos
ice cream cone
party hat
pyramid

Main Idea and Details

1 **What is the passage mainly about?**

  a. How to make some flat shapes.   **b.** Flat shapes and solid shapes.

  c. All kinds of solid shapes.   **d.** Plane figures around our homes.

2 **How many sides does a circle have?**

  a. None.   **b.** One.   **c.** Four.   **d.** Two.

3 **What does figures mean?**

  a. Flat shapes.   **b.** Plane shapes.   **c.** Solid shapes.   **d.** Regular shapes.

4 **Complete the sentences.**

  a. A _____ is a flat shape with three sides.

  b. The sides of a square are all the same _____ .

  c. Spheres and cubes are both _____ shapes.

  d. A _____ looks like a square but is solid.

5 **Complete the outline.**

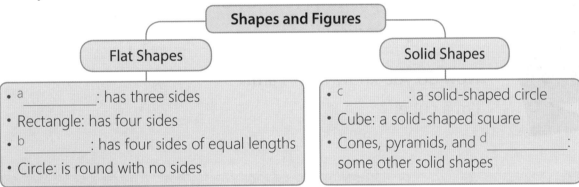

Shapes and Figures

Flat Shapes
- a _____: has three sides
- Rectangle: has four sides
- b _____: has four sides of equal lengths
- Circle: is round with no sides

Solid Shapes
- c _____: a solid-shaped circle
- Cube: a solid-shaped square
- Cones, pyramids, and d _____: some other solid shapes

Vocabulary Builder

Write the correct word and the meaning in Chinese.

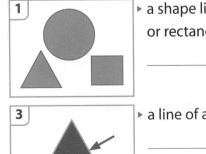
1 ▸ a shape like a triangle or rectangle

_____

2 ▸ a shape like a sphere or cube

_____

3 ▸ a line of a plane figure

_____

4 ▸ a shape with four sides

_____

What Am I?

  Let me tell you about myself.

I have six faces.

A face is a flat surface of a solid figure.

So I am a solid figure.

Key Words
- face
- flat surface
- intersect
- edge
- meet
- vertices
- vertex

My faces intersect at various points.

An edge is formed where two of my faces meet.

I have many edges.

I have twelve of them.

My faces also meet at different vertices.

A vertex is a point where three or more edges meet.

I have eight vertices.

Now do you know what I am?

I'm a cube!

✔ You can describe a solid figure by its number of faces, edges, and vertices.

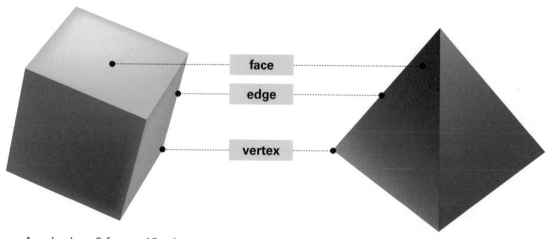

face

edge

vertex

A cube has 6 faces, 12 edges, and 8 vertices.

A pyramid has 5 faces, 8 edges, and 5 vertices.

Main Idea and Details

1 **What is the passage mainly about?**

    a. Where you can see a cube.   **b.** How a cube's faces intersect.

    c. How to draw a cube.   **d.** What a cube looks like.

2 **How many vertices does a cube have?**

    a. 6   **b.** 10   **c.** 12   **d.** 8

3 **What does intersect mean?**

    a. Draw.   **b.** Close.   **c.** Cross.   **d.** Point.

4 **According to the passage, which statement is true?**

    a. A cube has eight faces.

    b. A vertex is a flat surface of a solid shape.

    c. Two faces meet at an edge.

    d. A cube is a flat shape.

5 **Complete the outline.**

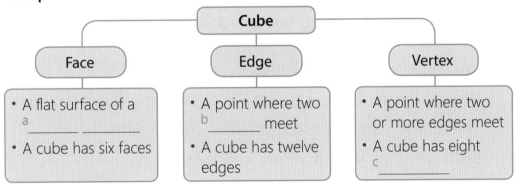

Cube

Face	Edge	Vertex
• A flat surface of a a _____ _____ • A cube has six faces	• A point where two b _____ meet • A cube has twelve edges	• A point where two or more edges meet • A cube has eight c _____

Vocabulary Builder

Write the correct word and the meaning in Chinese.

1  ▸ the line segment where two faces meet

_____

2  ▸ a flat surface of a solid figure

_____

3  ▸ a point where three or more edges meet

_____

4 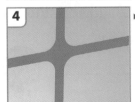 ▸ to pass across each other

_____

Counting Numbers

Key Words

- count
- number
- add
- count by tens
- count backward
- ordinal number
- order
- position
- end in

Let's count from 1 to 100.

One, two, three, four, five. Six, seven, eight, nine, ten.

What about the next ten numbers?

Eleven, twelve, thirteen, fourteen, fifteen.

Sixteen, seventeen, eighteen, nineteen, twenty.

How do we count higher than twenty?

First, we need to know these numbers:

Thirty, forty, fifty, sixty, seventy, eighty, and ninety.

After these words, just add a number from 1 to 9.

Now you can count to 100 (one hundred).

Let's practice counting by tens: 10, 20, 30, 40, 50, 60, 70, 80, 90.

Also, practice counting backward: 49, 48, 47, and so on.

We sometimes use ordinal numbers.

We use these numbers to tell the order or position of something.

The first ten are first, second, third, fourth, fifth.

Sixth, seventh, eighth, ninth, and tenth.

Except for first, second, and third, ordinal numbers end in "th."

Skip-counting by threes

1 2 ③ 4 5 ⑥ 7 8 ⑨ 10 11 ⑫ 13 14 ⑮ 16 17 ⑱ 19 20

✔ An ordinal number tells the order of an object or a person.

1st (first)	2nd (second)	3rd (third)	4th (fourth)	5th (fifth)

The girl is in the first position.
= The girl is first in line.

The dog is in the third position.
= The dog is third in line.

Main Idea and Details

1   **What is the passage mainly about?**

   a. Ordinal numbers.   **b.** Counting backward.

   c. Counting to one hundred.   **d.** Adding numbers.

2   **Which is an ordinal number?**

   a. Ten.   **b.** Eight.   **c.** Sixth.   **d.** Ninety.

3   **Use ordinal numbers to show the _____ of things.**

   a. Order.   **b.** Amount.   **c.** Value.   **d.** Length.

4   **According to the passage, which statement is true?**

   a. Ordinal numbers all end in "th."   **b.** People usually count with ordinal numbers.

   c. People cannot count backward.   **d.** You can add 1 to 9 to numbers like 30 and 40.

5   **Complete the outline.**

Counting Numbers	1 to 20	11 (eleven), 12 (ª_____), 13 (thirteen), 20 (twenty)
	21 to 100	21 (twenty-one) . . . 32 (ᵇ_____) . . . 87 (eighty-seven) . . . 100 (one hundred)
	Skip-Count	15 (fifteen), 25 (twenty-five), 35 (thirty-five), 45 (ᶜ_____)
	Count Backward	99 (ninety-nine), 98 (ninety-eight), 97 (ninety-seven), 96 (ninety-six)

Counting Ordinal Numbers	1st to 3rd	1st (first), 2nd (second), 3rd (ᵈ_____)
	After 3rd	4th (fourth), 5th (fifth) . . . 9th (ᵉ_____), 10th (tenth)

Vocabulary Builder

Write the correct word and the meaning in Chinese.

1   22, 21, 20, 19, 18...   ▸ to calculate in reverse order

_____

2   10, 20, 30, 40, 50...   ▸ to skip count by tens

_____

3   2 + 6   ▸ to put something with another thing

_____

4   1st, 2nd, 3rd, 4th, 5th...   ▸ a number that indicates the order or position of something

_____

Let's compare the values of numbers.

Key Words

- compare
- value
- number line
- more
- sign
- greater than
- less than
- equal to
- the same as

On a number line, a number that comes after another number is always 1 more.

For example, 6 is 1 more than 5.

So we can say, "6 is greater than 5."

Or we can write it like this: 6 > 5.

The sign **>** means "is greater than."

On a number line, a number that comes before another number is always 1 less.

For example, 3 is 1 less than 4.

So we can say, "3 is less than 4," or 3 < 4.

The sign **<** means "is less than."

Sometimes, two numbers have the same value.

For example, "3 is equal to 3."

We can write it like this: 3 = 3.

The sign **=** means "is equal to" or "is the same as."

✔ **Compare the numbers.**

6 is greater than 5.   6 > 5

3 is less than 4.   3 < 4

   =

3 is equal to 3.
3 is the same as 3.
3 = 3

Main Idea and Details

1   What is the passage mainly about?

a. Comparing the values of two numbers.

b. Why some numbers have the same value.

c. Showing that 2 is less than 5.

d. How signs are used to compare the values of numbers.

2   What is the symbol for "is less than"?

a. =   b. <   c. >   d. ≠

3   What does equal to mean?

a. The same as.   b. 1 more.   c. 1 less.   d. Greater than.

4   Complete the sentences.

a. A number that comes before another number is always 1 _____.

b. A number that comes after another number is always 1 _____.

c. 55 _____ than 40.

d. 12 _____ than 21.

5   Complete the outline.

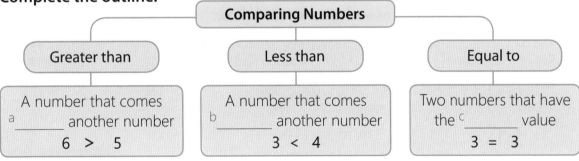

Comparing Numbers

Greater than	Less than	Equal to
A number that comes ᵃ_____ another number 6 > 5	A number that comes ᵇ_____ another number 3 < 4	Two numbers that have the ᶜ_____ value 3 = 3

Vocabulary Builder

Write the correct word and the meaning in Chinese.

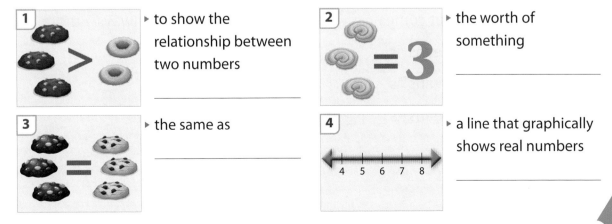

1 ► to show the relationship between two numbers
_____

2 ► the worth of something
_____

3 ► the same as
_____

4 ► a line that graphically shows real numbers
_____

A Complete the sentences with the words below.

triangle	intersect	edge	figure
sphere	flat surface	solid	vertex

1   A shape with three sides is called a _____.

2   A _____ is a regular shape.

3   A _____ is a solid-shaped circle.

4   Everywhere you look, you can see _____ shapes and figures.

5   A face is a _____ _____ of a solid figure.

6   My faces _____ at various points.

7   An _____ is formed where two of my faces meet.

8   A _____ is a point where three or more edges meet.

B Complete the sentences with the words below.

ordinal numbers	count	by tens	less
backward	equal	greater	after

1   Let's _____ from 1 to 100.

2   Let's practice counting _____ _____ : 10, 20, 30, 40, 50, 60, 70, 80, 90.

3   Also, practice counting _____ : 49, 48, 47, and so on.

4   We use _____ _____ to tell the order or position of something.

5   A number that comes _____ another number is always 1 more.

6   The sign > means "is _____ than."

7   The sign < means "is _____ than."

8   The sign = means "is _____ to" or "is the same as."

Write the correct word and the meaning in Chinese.

1 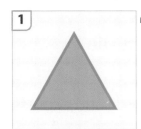 ▸ a shape with three sides

_____

2 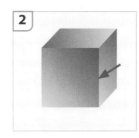 ▸ the line segment where two faces meet

_____

3  ▸ a shape that is wide near the bottom and narrows gradually to the top

_____

4  ▸ a point where three or more edges meet

_____

5 1st, 2nd, 3rd, 4th, 5th... ▸ a number that indicates the order or position of something

_____

6 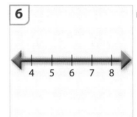 ▸ a line that graphically shows real numbers

_____

D

Match each word with the correct definition and write the meaning in Chinese.

1 solid shape _____ ☐

2 side _____ ☐

3 rectangle _____ ☐

4 flat surface_____ ☐

5 count backward _____ ☐

6 order _____ ☐

7 square _____ ☐

8 value _____ ☐

9 sign _____ ☐

10 compare _____ ☐

a. a shape with four sides of equal length

b. the worth of something

c. a line of a plane figure

d. a shape with four sides

e. to calculate in reverse order

f. a smooth, level surface

g. a shape like a sphere or cube

h. lettering or symbols of something

i. the correct position of two or more numbers

j. to show the relationship between two numbers

Being a Good Writer

Key Words

- **grammar**
- **punctuation**
- **punctuation mark**
- **capitalization**
- **capital letter**
- **capitalize**
- **period**
- **exclamation point**

A good writer uses good grammar and punctuation.

Grammar is the rules of a language.

When you write a sentence, use the correct words and expressions.

Also, use proper punctuation marks to show where the sentence stops.

Here are a few rules for writing.

Capitalization:

1. Use a capital letter at the beginning of a sentence.

2. The word "I" is always a capital letter.

3. The names of people or special places should begin with a capital letter.

4. Capitalize the names of the days of the week, months, and holidays.

Punctuation:

1. Use a period to end a sentence.

2. All questions need a question mark.

3. To show surprise or excitement, use an exclamation point.

4. Use a comma between each person, place, thing, or phrase in a list.

✔ Checklist for Good Writing

Capitalize:

- at the beginning of each sentence
- the word "I"
- names of people and places
- days of the week, months, and holidays

Use proper punctuation marks:

- period   ▪ → Let's go.
- question mark   ? → Do you like winter?
- exclamation point ! → Great!
- commas   , → I like apples, pears, and bananas.

Main Idea and Details

1 **What is the main idea of the passage?**

a. Capitalization and punctuation are important. **b.** Every language has rules.

c. You should always capitalize some words in English. **d.** Try to be a good writer.

2 **What is grammar?**

a. Punctuation. **b.** Capital letters.

c. The rules of a language. **d.** Correct words and expressions.

3 **What does proper mean?**

a. Different. **b.** Important. **c.** Special. **d.** Correct.

4 **Complete the sentences.**

a. It is important to _____ the names of months.

b. End a sentence with a _____.

c. You can show excitement with an _____ _____.

5 **Complete the outline.**

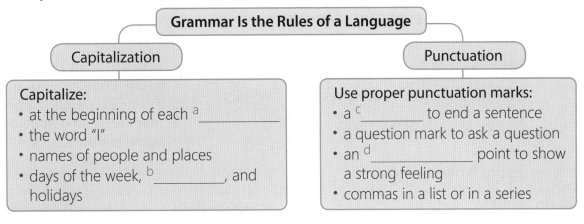

Grammar Is the Rules of a Language

Capitalization

Capitalize:
• at the beginning of each ᵃ_____
• the word "I"
• names of people and places
• days of the week, ᵇ_____, and holidays

Punctuation

Use proper punctuation marks:
• a ᶜ_____ to end a sentence
• a question mark to ask a question
• an ᵈ_____ point to show a strong feeling
• commas in a list or in a series

Vocabulary Builder

Write the correct word and the meaning in Chinese.

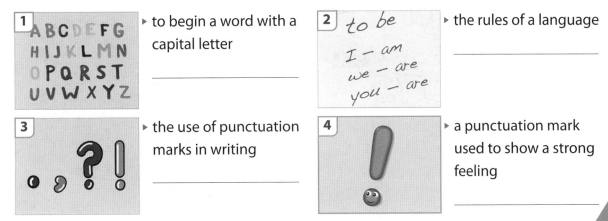

1 A B C D E F G H I J K L M N O P Q R S T U V W X Y Z
▸ to begin a word with a capital letter
_____

2 to be
I – am
we – are
you – are
▸ the rules of a language
_____

3 ？ !
▸ the use of punctuation marks in writing
_____

4 !
▸ a punctuation mark used to show a strong feeling
_____

1 ——— August 5, 2017

2 ——— Dear Sarah,

How are you doing?
Everything is fine with me.

I am having a great summer with my family.
We stayed at Palm Beach for one week.
3 — I went swimming and fishing.
One day, we even did some snorkeling!

How is your summer vacation going?
School is going to begin in two weeks.
I'll see you in class soon.

4 ——— Yours truly,
Tom

1 **Date:** Write the date at the top. Use a capital letter for the name of the month. When you write a date, put a comma between the day and year.

2 **Greeting:** Start greetings with "Dear" and your friend's name. Use a capital letter. Put a comma after the greeting.

3 **Body:** The body of the letter is what you want to write. Use capital letters at the beginning of each sentence.

4 **Closing:** End the letter with a closing and your name. Put a comma after the closing. Don't forget that the closing and your name should start with capital letters.

***Capitalization:** Capitalize the names of people and special places.

***Punctuation:** Use proper punctuation marks. Check the periods, commas, question marks, and exclamation points in the letter.

fishing

snorkeling

Main Idea and Details

1 **What is the main idea of the passage?**

a. School is starting soon.

b. The boy is having a great vacation.

c. Sarah went to Palm Beach.

d. Tom will meet Sarah in class.

2 **What should you write in the body of a letter?**

a. A greeting.　　　　　b. What you want to tell.

c. The date.　　　　　　d. Your name.

3 **What does vacation mean?**

a. Break.　　　b. Class.　　　c. Trip.　　　d. Week.

4 **Answer the questions.**

a. What do you put between the date and the year?　_____

b. How do you begin a greeting?　_____

c. How should you begin every sentence?　_____

5 **Complete the outline.**

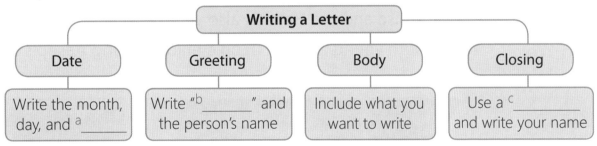

Writing a Letter

Date	Greeting	Body	Closing
Write the month, day, and ª_____	Write "ᵇ_____" and the person's name	Include what you want to write	Use a ᶜ_____ and write your name

Vocabulary Builder

Write the correct word and the meaning in Chinese.

 **1** ▸ warm; showing friendship

_____

 **2** ▸ an expression of friendly regard

_____

 **3** ▸ a phrase used at the end of a letter

_____

 **4** ▸ the main part of a letter

_____

85

Aesop's Fables

Key Words

- Aesop
- slave
- storyteller
- make up
- fable
- lesson
- character
- moral

A long time ago, a man lived on the Greek island of Samos.

His name was Aesop, and he was a slave.

But he was also a great storyteller.

Aesop often made up stories to tell people.

His stories were called fables.

A fable is a short story that teaches people a lesson.

Animals are often the main characters.

The animals talk and act like people.

At the end of the fable, Aesop always tells the reader a lesson.

The lesson is called the moral of the story.

Aesop wrote many famous fables.

"The Ant and the Grasshopper" is one of them.

"The Tortoise and the Hare" is also very popular.

Today, both young and old people enjoy reading Aesop's fables.

Animals are the main characters in Aesop's fables.

Fables always end with a moral lesson.

The Tortoise and the Hare

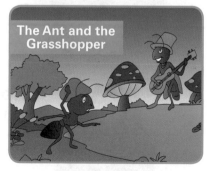

The Ant and the Grasshopper

Main Idea and Details

1 **What is the main idea of the passage?**

a. Fables are usually stories about animals.

b. People still read Aesop's fables today.

c. Aesop told many fables with a moral lesson.

d. Animals in a fable talk and act like people.

2 **What does famous mean?**

a. Important. **b.** Interesting. **c.** Well-known. **d.** Great.

3 **The main _____ in fables are often animals.**

a. Lessons. **b.** Characters. **c.** Stories. **d.** Storytellers.

4 **According to the passage, which statement is true?**

a. Aesop used to talk to animals.

b. Aesop lived in Greece a few years ago.

c. Aesop told stories with moral lessons.

d. Aesop was once a prince.

5 **Complete the outline.**

Aesop

Aesop's Life
- Lived on the ᵃ_____ island of Samos
- Was a slave
- Made up ᵇ_____ to tell people

Aesop's Fables
- Short stories with a ᶜ_____ lesson
- Often have talking animals
- "The ᵈ_____ and the Grasshopper" and "The Tortoise and the Hare" are still famous.

Vocabulary Builder

Write the correct word and the meaning in Chinese.

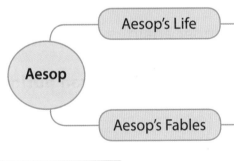

1 ▸ a short story that teaches people a lesson

_____

2 ▸ someone who tells or writes stories

_____

3 ▸ a person in a book, drama, or movie

_____

4 ▸ a lesson in a fable

_____

Key Words

- field
- ant
- gather
- grasshopper
- meal
- shiver
- prepare

An ant and a grasshopper once lived in the same field.

Every day, the ant worked hard and gathered food for winter.

But the grasshopper just played and sang all summer long.

Summer changed to fall, and the weather became colder.

The ant started working even harder than before.

But the grasshopper still played and played.

One day, the first snow fell.

The ant went inside and ate a nice, warm meal.

Meanwhile, the grasshopper started shivering from the cold.

"I'm cold and hungry. What shall I do?" he said.

When spring came, the weather became warmer.

So the ant went outside.

But the ant never saw the grasshopper again.

Moral: Don't forget to prepare for bad times even during good times.

Main Idea and Details

1   What is the passage mainly about?

a. A very cold winter.

b. An ant and a grasshopper.

c. A fight between an ant and a grasshopper.

d. A good time in the field.

2   What did the grasshopper do in summer?

a. He played.   **b.** He gathered food.   **c.** He ate warm meals.   **d.** He disappeared.

3   What does shivering mean?

a. Shaking.   **b.** Eating.   **c.** Running.   **d.** Waking.

4   Complete the sentences.

a. In summer, the ant worked _____ every day.

b. The grasshopper played and _____ during summer.

c. The ant never saw the grasshopper after _____ ended.

5   Complete the outline.

> **The Ant and the Grasshopper**

> **The Ant**
> - Worked hard gathering ᵃ_____
> - Went inside home in winter
> - Enjoyed nice warm ᵇ_____
> - Never saw the grasshopper again

> **The Grasshopper**
> - Played and sang during summer
> - ᶜ_____ in the cold when winter came
> - Was cold and ᵈ_____
> - Was never seen again

Vocabulary Builder

Write the correct word and the meaning in Chinese.

1  ▸ to collect; to bring or come together in one place

_____

2  ▸ an open area of land

_____

3  ▸ to shake or tremble from the cold or fear

_____

4  ▸ a plant-eating insect with long legs used for jumping

_____

A

Complete the sentences with the words below.

capitalize	grammar	sentence	body
proper	vacation	greetings	period

1   A good writer uses good _____ and punctuation.

2   Use a capital letter at the beginning of a _____.

3   _____ the names of the days of the week, months, and holidays.

4   Use a _____ to end a sentence.

5   Use _____ punctuation marks to show where the sentence stops.

6   Start _____ with "Dear" and your friend's name.

7   The _____ of letter is what you want to write.

8   How is your summer _____ going?

B

Complete the sentences with the words below.

famous	grasshopper	fable	made up
harder	shivering	moral	prepare for

1   Aesop often _____ _____ stories to tell people.

2   Aesop wrote many _____ fables.

3   A _____ is a short story that teaches people a lesson.

4   Aesop always tells the reader a lesson called a _____.

5   An ant and a _____ once lived in the same field.

6   The ant started working even _____ than before.

7   Meanwhile, the grasshopper started _____ from the cold.

8   Don't forget to _____ _____ bad times even during good times.

Write the correct word and the meaning in Chinese.

1 ▸ to collect; to bring or come together in one place

_____

2 ▸ the sport of swimming with a snorkel and a face mask

_____

3 ▸ a sign such as a period, comma, or question mark

_____

4 ▸ a short story that teaches people a lesson

_____

5 ▸ a person in a book, drama, or movie

_____

6 ▸ breakfast, lunch, or dinner

_____

D

Match each word with the correct definition and write the meaning in Chinese.

1 capitalize _____ ☐

2 capitalization _____ ☐

3 excitement _____ ☐

4 friendly _____ ☐

5 slave _____ ☐

6 storyteller _____ ☐

7 moral _____ ☐

8 gather _____ ☐

9 prepare _____ ☐

10 shiver _____ ☐

a. to shake or tremble from the cold or fear

b. to begin a word with a capital letter

c. warm; showing friendship

d. the use of capital letters in writing or printing

e. an excited state or condition

f. someone who is owned by another person and works for him

g. to get ready

h. someone who tells or writes stories

i. to collect; to bring or come together in one place

j. a lesson in a fable

Kinds of Paintings

Key Words
- artist
- create
- painting
- landscape
- scenery
- still life
- works
- portrait
- self-portrait

Artists create many different kinds of paintings.

Some artists like to paint landscapes.
The most important thing in a landscape is the scenery.
It often includes the land, the trees, the sky, lakes, and rivers.
The weather, season, and time of the day are also very important.

Some artists like to paint still lifes.
The objects in a still life do not move.
That is why it is called a still life.
To paint a still life, an artist has to prepare the objects to paint.
Still lifes often include fruits, flowers, and other small objects.

Paintings of people are other common works.
A painting of a person is called a portrait.
A self-portrait is a portrait of the artist himself.

landscape

still life

Mona Lisa by Leonardo da Vinci, the most famous portrait in the world

Vincent van Gogh painted many self-portraits.

Main Idea and Details

1 What is the passage mainly about?

a. Painting skills of landscapes.   b. People's favorite paintings.

c. Portraits and self-portraits.   d. Different types of paintings.

2 What is a self-portrait?

a. A painting of something that does not move.

b. A painting that shows the artist himself.

c. A painting that shows outdoor scenery.

d. A painting of a famous person.

3 What does objects mean?

a. Pictures.   b. Things.   c. Paints.   d. Works.

4 According to the passage, which statement is true?

a. A landscape often includes fruits and flowers.

b. A still life is a picture of the artist himself.

c. A portrait shows a person in the painting.

d. The weather and season are important to a self-portrait.

5 Complete the outline.

A Kind of Painting

Landscape	Still Life	Portrait
A painting of ᵃ _____ like the land, the trees, the sky, lakes, and rivers	A painting of ᵇ _____ that do not move, like fruits and flowers	A painting of a ᶜ _____

Vocabulary Builder

Write the correct word and the meaning in Chinese.

 **1** ▸ a picture of the scenery

_____

 **2** ▸ someone who makes paintings, sculptures, etc.

_____

3 ▸ a painting of objects like fruits and flowers

_____

 **4** ▸ a picture of the artist himself or herself

_____

Key Words

- materials
- easel
- oil paint
- popular
- painter
- vivid
- prefer
- watercolor
- finger paint
- charcoal

Artists need special materials to make their pictures.
They need drawing materials, paints, brushes,
a canvas, and an easel.

There are several kinds of paint.
Oil paints are popular with many painters.
Oil paints produce rich and vivid colors on the pictures.
Other artists prefer to use watercolors and finger paints.
Watercolor pictures are often very bright.
Finger paints produce unique and fun pictures.

There are many kinds of drawing materials.
Of course, some artists just use simple pencils.
But others use color pencils to brighten their pictures.
Some prefer crayons, which also come in many colors.
And a few artists draw pictures with charcoal.
All of these drawing materials can produce great pictures.

✔ Types of Painting

oil painting

watercolor painting

finger painting

Finger paints create unique and fun pictures.

✔ Drawing materials

pencils

color pencils

crayons

charcoal

Main Idea and Details

brush
paint

1 **What is the main idea of the passage?**

a. Most artists use oil paints.

b. Artists can draw with pencils or charcoal.

c. Artists need paint or drawing materials.

d. Few artists prefer to use finger paints.

2 **What drawing material can make bright pictures?**

a. Finger paints. **b.** Charcoal. **c.** Color pencils. **d.** Simple pencils.

3 **What does vivid mean?**

a. Boring. **b.** Colorful. **c.** Pretty. **d.** Unique.

4 **Complete the sentences.**

a. All artists need special _____ to make pictures.

b. Artists can make fun pictures with _____ paints.

c. There are many _____ of crayons.

5 **Complete the outline.**

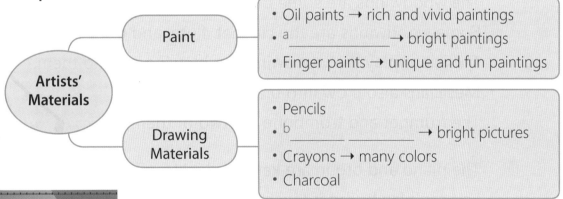

Artists' Materials

Paint
- Oil paints → rich and vivid paintings
- a _____ → bright paintings
- Finger paints → unique and fun paintings

Drawing Materials
- Pencils
- b _____ _____ → bright pictures
- Crayons → many colors
- Charcoal

Vocabulary Builder

Write the correct word and the meaning in Chinese.

 **1** ▸ an artist who paints pictures

_____

 **2** ▸ a frame for supporting an artist's painting

_____

 **3** ▸ very bright in color

_____

 **4** ▸ things such as pencils, crayons, and charcoal

_____

95

There are different kinds of musical instruments.

Key Words

- **musical instrument**
- **string**
- **bow**
- **pluck**
- **percussion**
- **woodwind**
- **brass**
- **keyboard**

Let's meet the string family.

Can you name some instruments with strings?

The violin? The cello? How about the guitar?

You usually use bows to play string instruments.

But sometimes you pluck the strings with your fingers.

Let's meet the percussion family.

These include the drum, xylophone, and tambourine.

Percussion instruments are fun to play.

You hit them or shake them with your hands or a stick.

The woodwinds are some other common instruments.

Some woodwinds are the clarinet, flute, and oboe.

Musicians play the woodwinds by blowing air into them.

Musicians also blow into brass instruments.

The trumpet and trombone are two of them.

The piano and organ are keyboard instruments.

You can play keyboard instruments by using your fingers.

string instruments

guitar   violin

woodwind instruments

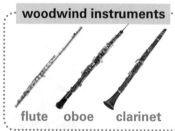

flute   oboe   clarinet

brass instruments

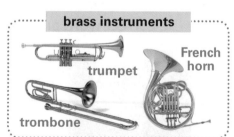

trumpet   French horn

trombone

percussion instruments

tambourine

drum   cymbals   xylophone

keyboard instruments

piano

organ

Main Idea and Details

1   **What is the passage mainly about?**

   a. The sounds musical instruments make.   **b.** How to play some musical instruments.

   c. Different kinds of musical instruments.   **d.** Popular instruments among musicians.

2   **What family is the clarinet in?**

   a. The percussion family.   **b.** The brass family.

   c. The woodwind family.   **d.** The keyboard family.

3   **What does pluck mean?**

   a. Pull.   **b.** Cut.   **c.** Hit.   **d.** Shake.

4   **Complete the sentences.**

   a. The violin belongs to the _____ family.

   b. The xylophone is a _____ instrument.

   c. Musicians have to _____ on flutes to play them.

5   **Complete the outline.**

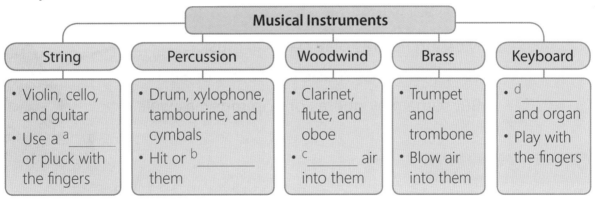

Musical Instruments

String	Percussion	Woodwind	Brass	Keyboard
• Violin, cello, and guitar • Use a ^a_____ or pluck with the fingers	• Drum, xylophone, tambourine, and cymbals • Hit or ^b_____ them	• Clarinet, flute, and oboe • ^c_____ air into them	• Trumpet and trombone • Blow air into them	• ^d_____ and organ • Play with the fingers

Vocabulary Builder

Write the correct word and the meaning in Chinese.

1 ▸ a tool for producing a musical sound

_____

2 ▸ instruments like the drum and tambourine

_____

3 ▸ a person who writes music or plays a musical instrument

_____

4 ▸ instruments like the piano and organ

_____

  36

Key Words

- attend
- concert
- orchestra
- conductor
- conduct
- harmony
- classical music
- opera

Have you ever attended a concert?

Or have you ever watched an orchestra on television?

All of the musical instruments come together in an orchestra.

String, percussion, woodwind, brass, and keyboard instruments make up an orchestra.

The musicians all play together, and they make beautiful music.

The conductor leads the orchestra.

He or she stands in front of the orchestra and conducts the music.

The conductor makes sure that all the members do their jobs at the right time.

This lets them play in harmony.

Most orchestras play classical music.

They might play music by Mozart or Bach.

But some play operas or pop music as well.

✓ **The Orchestra**

horn   trumpet   trombone   tuba

clarinet   bassoon

flute   oboe

percussion   bass

violin   viola

violin   cello

Main Idea and Details

1   What is the main idea of the passage?

a. Orchestras usually play classical music.

b. There are many instruments in an orchestra.

c. An orchestra always has string instruments.

d. The conductor is the most important person in an orchestra.

2   What does the conductor do?

a. Plays musical instruments.   **b.** Writes the music.

c. Holds concerts.   **d.** Leads the musicians.

3   What does make up mean?

a. Form.   **b.** Invent.   **c.** Play.   **d.** Attend.

4   Answer the questions.

a. What families of instruments make up an orchestra?

_____

b. Who stands in front of the orchestra?   _____

c. What kind of music do most orchestras play?   _____

5   Complete the outline.

Orchestras

Musical Instruments	Conductor	Types of Music
• All of the musical instruments: string, percussion, ᵃ _____, brass, and keyboard instruments	• Leads the musicians • Makes them play in ᵇ _____	• Mostly ᶜ _____ music • Also opera and pop music

Vocabulary Builder

Write the correct word and the meaning in Chinese.

 ▸ a group of musicians who play together on different instruments

_____

▸ serious music written by people such as Mozart and Beethoven

_____

 ▸ a person who leads the orchestra

_____

▸ a type of play performed by singers and an orchestra

_____

A

Complete the sentences with the words below.

oil paints	materials	still life	paintings
self-portrait	drawing	scenery	watercolor

1 Artists create many different kinds of _____.

2 The most important thing in a landscape is the _____.

3 The objects in a _____ _____ do not move.

4 A _____ is a portrait of the artist himself.

5 Artists need special _____ to make their pictures.

6 _____ _____ are popular with many painters.

7 _____ pictures are often very bright.

8 All of these _____ materials can produce great pictures.

B

Complete the sentences with the words below.

instruments	classical	string	blowing
woodwinds	leads	orchestra	attended

1 There are different kinds of musical _____.

2 You usually use bows to play _____ instruments.

3 Musicians play the woodwinds by _____ air into them.

4 Some _____ are the clarinet, flute, and oboe.

5 Have you ever _____ a concert?

6 All of the musical instruments come together in an _____.

7 The conductor _____ the orchestra.

8 Most orchestras play _____ music.

Write the correct word and the meaning in Chinese.

 **1** ▸ a type of paint that is mixed with water

_____

 **2** ▸ a view of natural features

_____

 **3** ▸ a painting of objects like fruits and flowers

_____

 **4** ▸ a musical performance given in public

_____

 **5** ▸ instruments using bows to play

_____

 **6** ▸ a person who leads the orchestra

_____

D

Match each word with the correct definition and write the meaning in Chinese.

1 painter _____ ☐

2 popular _____ ☐

3 prefer _____ ☐

4 drawing materials _____ ☐

5 percussion (instruments) _____ ☐

6 musical instrument _____ ☐

7 brass (instruments) _____ ☐

8 orchestra _____ ☐

9 attend _____ ☐

10 conduct _____ ☐

a. to direct; to lead

b. things such as pencils, crayons, and charcoal

c. liked or enjoyed by most people

d. to like something better than another

e. to go to an event

f. a tool for producing a musical sound

g. instruments like the trumpet and trombone

h. a group of musicians who play together on different instruments

i. an artist who paints pictures

j. instruments like the drum and tambourine

Wrap-Up Test 3

A Write the correct word for each sentence.

> fables   flat shapes   solid shapes   greater   musical
> grammar   bad times   oil paints   the same   capitalize

1 Triangles, rectangles, circles are called _____ _____.

2 Cones, pyramids, and cylinders are _____ _____.

3 The sign > means "is _____ than."

4 The sign = means "is equal to" or "is _____ _____ as."

5 A good writer uses good _____ and punctuation.

6 _____ the names of the days of the week, months, and holidays.

7 Aesop wrote many famous _____.

8 Don't forget to prepare for _____ _____ even during good times.

9 There are different kinds of _____ instruments.

10 _____ _____ produce rich and vivid colors on the pictures.

B Write the meanings of the words in Chinese.

1	plane figure	_____	16	fable	_____
2	solid figure	_____	17	character	_____
3	side	_____	18	meal	_____
4	face	_____	19	moral	_____
5	vertex	_____	20	grasshopper	_____
6	rectangle	_____	21	portrait	_____
7	cone	_____	22	landscape	_____
8	sphere	_____	23	still life	_____
9	ordinal number	_____	24	paint	_____
10	number line	_____	25	drawing materials	_____
11	capitalize	_____	26	prefer	_____
12	capitalization	_____	27	unique	_____
13	capital letter	_____	28	percussion instruments	_____
14	punctuation mark	_____	29	woodwind instruments	_____
15	friendly	_____	30	brass instruments	_____

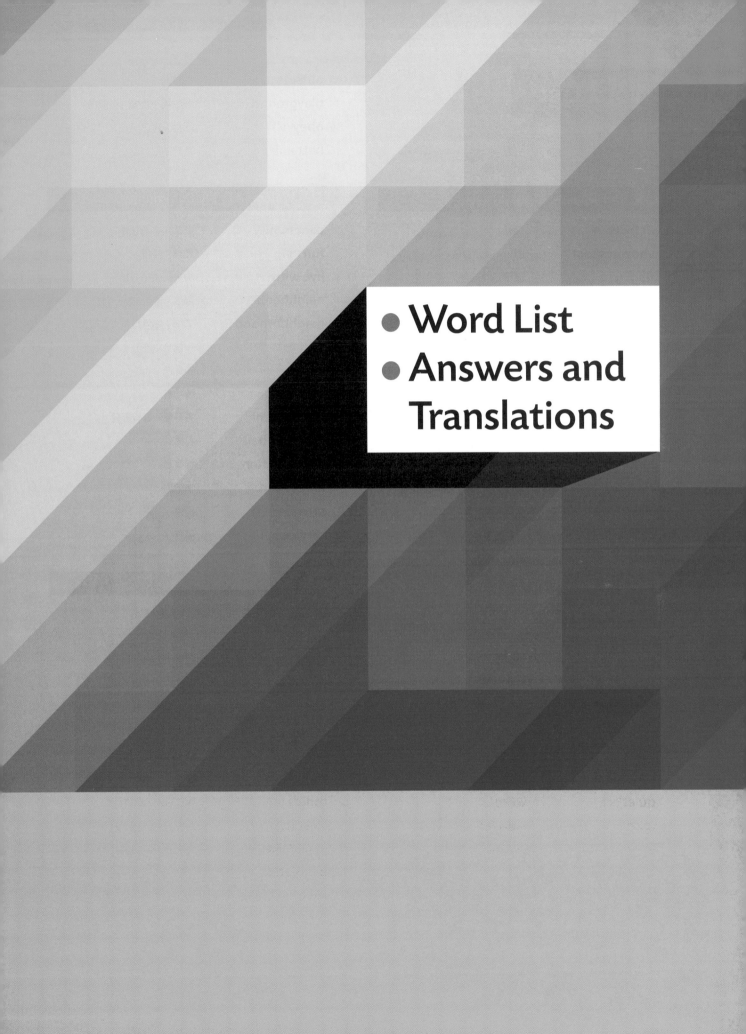

- Word List
- Answers and Translations

Word List

13 **outside** (adv.)　　在外面
14 **playground** (n.)　　運動場；操場；遊樂場
15 **obey** (v.)　　服從；遵守
16 **better** (a.)　　更好的

01　Our Day at School

1 **activity** (n.)　　活動
2 **show respect**　　對……表示尊敬
3 **flag** (n.)　　旗子
4 **stand up**　　起立
5 **face** (v.)　　面對；面向
6 **put** (v.)　　放；擺
7 **Pledge of Allegiance**　　（美國）效忠國家的宣誓
8 **subject** (n.)　　科目；學科
9 **how to**　　（指方式、方法）怎樣；怎麼
10 **solve** (v.)　　解答（數學題）
11 **math problem**　　數學題
12 **class** (n.)　　班級；（一節）課；上課
13 **classmate** (n.)　　同班同學
14 **cafeteria** (n.)　　自助餐廳
15 **get** (v.)　　獲得；得到
16 **get along**　　和睦相處

02　School Rules

1 **rule** (n.)　　規則
2 **follow** (v.)　　遵守
3 **one another**　　彼此；互相
4 **stay** (v.)　　繼續；保持
5 **safe** (a.)　　安全的
6 **classroom** (n.)　　教室
7 **quiet** (a.)　　安靜的
8 **raise** (v.)　　舉起；抬起
9 **yell** (v.)　　叫喊；吼叫
10 **fight** (v.)　　打架；爭吵
*動詞三態
fight–fought–fought
11 **each other**　　互相
12 **hallway** (n.)　　走廊

03　Welcome to My Community

1 **community** (n.)　　社區；共同社會
2 **fun** (n.)　　娛樂；樂趣
3 **live with**　　與……住在一起
4 **neighbor** (n.)　　鄰居；鄰近的人(或物)
5 **neighborhood** (n.)　　近鄰；鄰近地區；整個街坊
6 **part** (n.)　　一部分；部分
7 **pool** (n.)　　游泳池
8 **museum** (n.)　　博物館
9 **have a picnic**　　去野餐；舉行野餐
10 **play baseball**　　打棒球
11 **police station**　　警察局
12 **fire station**　　消防局
13 **provide** (v.)　　提供
14 **service** (n.)　　服務

04　Being a Good Citizen

1 **live in**　　住在……
2 **need to**　　需要；必要
3 **citizen** (n.)　　市民；公民
4 **member** (n.)　　成員
5 **state** (n.)　　（美國的）州
6 **country** (n.)　　國家；國土
7 **way** (n.)　　路；方法；方式
8 **respect** (v.)　　尊敬
9 **others** (n.)　　其它的人（或物）
10 **treat** (v.)　　對待
11 **would like to**　　想要……
12 **be treated**　　被對待
13 **keep** (v.)　　持有；保有
14 **care for**　　關心；照顧

05 Celebrating Holidays

1	**celebrate** (v.)	慶祝；過節
2	**holiday** (n.)	節日；假日
3	**special** (a.)	特別的
4	**honor** (v.)	尊敬；敬重；給予（某人）以……的榮譽
5	**event** (n.)	事件；大事
6	**national holiday**	國定假日
7	**fly** (v.)	懸掛（旗）；升（旗）
8	Martin Luther King, Jr. Day	馬丁·路德·金恩紀念日
9	**be celebrated**	被慶祝
10	**African-American**	非裔美國人
11	**Memorial Day**	（美國）陣亡將士紀念日
12	**Veterans Day**	（美國）退伍軍人節
13	**independence** (n.)	獨立
14	**Independence Day**	（美國）獨立紀念日
15	**fireworks** (n.)	煙火；放煙火；煙火大會
16	**Labor Day**	（美國）勞動節

06 Holiday Traditions

1	**tradition** (n.)	傳統
2	**repeat** (v.)	重複；重做
3	**year after year**	每年；年復一年
4	**Mother's Day**	母親節
5	**present (= gift)** (n.)	禮物
6	**Valentine's Day**	情人節
7	**dress up**	裝扮
8	**scary** (a.)	嚇人的
9	**costume** (n.)	（特定場合之）服裝；裝束
10	**Halloween** (n.)	萬聖節前夕（10月31日）
11	**trick-or-treat**	不給糖就搗蛋 *指萬聖節孩童們挨家逐戶要糖果的遊戲
12	**Chinese New Year**	中國新年；春節；農曆新年
13	**get together**	聚集；聚會
14	**Thanksgiving** (n.)	= Thanksgiving Day 感恩節
15	**decorate** (v.)	裝飾
16	**dinner** (n.)	晚餐；晚宴

07 America's Symbols

1	**symbol** (n.)	符號；象徵
2	**object** (n.)	物體
3	**stand for**	代表；象徵；意味著
4	**Liberty Bell**	自由鐘
5	**freedom** (n.)	自由；獨立自主
6	**ring** (v.)	按鈴；搖鈴；敲鐘 *動詞三態 ring–rang–rung
7	**announce** (v.)	宣布；發布
8	**bald eagle**	白頭鷹
9	**symbolize** (v.)	象徵；標誌
10	**Statue of Liberty**	自由女神像
11	**statue** (n.)	雕像；塑像
12	**stand** (v.)	站立；立定
13	**in the middle of**	在……中間；在……中途
14	**New York Harbor**	紐約港
15	**welcome** (v.)	歡迎；接待
16	**Uncle Sam**	山姆大叔（美國政府的綽號）*原為美國一位肉類包裝商之名，後因「山姆大叔」與「美國」的縮寫都是U.S.，故常被用來代指美國或美國政府。

08 National Flags

1	**national** (a.)	全國性的；國家的
2	**national flag**	國旗
3	**American** (a.)	美國的
4	**Stars and Stripes**	星條旗
5	**stripe** (n.)	條紋；線條
6	**represent** (v.)	象徵；表示
7	**current** (a.)	現時的；當前的
8	**northern** (a.)	（在）北方的；向北方的；來自北方的
9	**Canadian** (a.)	加拿大的
10	**maple leaf**	楓葉
11	**maple** (n.)	楓樹
12	**southern** (a.)	（在）南方的；向南方的
13	**Mexican** (a.)	墨西哥的

14	**eagle** (n.)	老鷹
15	**snake** (n.)	蛇
16	**cactus** (n.)	仙人掌

09 America's Capital

1	**capital** (n.)	首都；首府
2	**leader** (n.)	領袖；領導者
3	**president** (n.)	總統
4	**lead** (v.)	領導；指揮；率領
5	**work with**	與……共事；與……協作
6	**government** (n.)	政府
7	**state** (n.)	州
8	**capital city**	國府；州府
9	**Arizona** (n.)	美國亞利桑那州
10	**Hawaii** (n.)	美國夏威夷州
11	**governor** (n.)	州長
12	**state capital**	州府

10 Washington D.C.

1	**national government**	（尤指非常時期成立的）聯合政府；國民聯合政府
2	**White House**	白宮（美國總統官邸）
3	**Capitol** (n.)	（美國）國會大廈
4	**make laws**	制定法律
5	**dome** (n.)	圓屋頂；圓蓋
6	**style** (n.)	風格；作風；樣式；類型
7	**capitol** (n.)	（美國）州議會大廈
8	**Supreme Court**	最高法院
9	**judge** (n.)	法官；裁判
10	**court** (n.)	法庭；法院
11	**decide** (v.)	決定；裁決；判決
12	**be broken**	被打破；被違反；被損壞 *動詞三態 break–broke–broken
13	**Washington Monument**	華盛頓紀念碑
14	**monument** (n.)	紀念碑；紀念塔；紀念館

11 Our Land and Water

1	**shape** (n.)	形狀；外形
2	**land** (n.)	陸地；土地
3	**be called**	被叫做；被視為……
4	**landform** (n.)	地形
5	**form** (n.)	形狀；外形；種類；類型
6	**as high as**	像……一樣高；像……那麼高
7	**valley** (n.)	山谷；溪谷
8	**be covered with**	被……覆蓋
9	**kind** (n.)	種類；性質
10	**plain** (n.)	平地；平原；曠野
11	**flat** (a.)	平的；平坦的
12	**be surrounded by**	被……包圍；被……環繞
13	**ocean** (n.)	海洋；海
14	**island** (n.)	島
15	**surface** (n.)	表面
16	**flow into**	流入

12 Where in the World Do We Live?

1	**continent** (n.)	大陸；大洲
2	**piece** (n.)	一個；一張；一片；一塊
3	**name** (v.)	列舉；陳說；說出……的名字
4	**Asia** (n.)	亞洲
5	**Africa** (n.)	非洲
6	**Australia** (n.)	澳洲
7	**Europe** (n.)	歐洲
8	**Antarctica** (n.)	南極洲
9	**North America**	北美洲
10	**South America**	南美洲
11	**largest** (a.)	最大的；最廣泛的 *原級 – 比較級 – 最高級 large（大的）– larger（比較大的）– largest（最大的）
12	**on Earth**	地球上；世界上
13	**coldest** (a.)	最冷的；最寒冷的 *原級 – 比較級 – 最高級 cold（寒冷的）– colder（比較寒冷的）– coldest（最寒冷的）
14	**Old World**	舊大陸
15	**New World**	新大陸

16	Pacific Ocean	太平洋
17	Atlantic Ocean	大西洋
18	Indian Ocean	印度洋
19	Arctic Ocean	北冰洋
20	Antarctic Ocean	南冰洋
21	be located in	位於；座落於
22	next to	緊鄰著

13 Parts of Plants

1	part (n.)	部位；部分
2	need (v.)	需要；有……必要
3	absorb (v.)	吸收（液體、氣體、光、聲等）
4	nutrient (n.)	營養物
5	soil (n.)	土；土壤
6	root (n.)	（植物的）根；地下莖
7	hold (v.)	保持；支撐
8	ground (n.)	土壤；土地；地面
9	stem (n.)	莖；（樹）幹；（葉）柄
10	support (v.)	支撐
11	leaf (n.)	葉子
12	flower (n.)	花
13	carry (v.)	運送；運載；搬運
14	air (n.)	空氣
15	seed (n.)	籽；種子
16	grow into	成長為……

14 What Do Plants Need?

1	try to	試圖；嘗試
2	grow (v.)	生長；發育
3	probably (adv.)	大概；或許；很可能
4	realize (v.)	領悟；了解；認識到
5	rain (n.)	雨
6	without (prep.)	無；沒有；不
7	die (v.)	（草木等）枯萎；凋謝
8	contain (v.)	包含；容納
9	as well	也；同樣地
10	take in	讓……進入；接受；吸收
11	finally (adv.)	最後；終於

12	space (n.)	空間
13	healthy (a.)	健康的
14	get bigger	變大
15	room (n.)	房間
16	grow bigger	長大

15 Where Do Animals Live?

1	polar bear	北極熊
2	desert (n.)	沙漠
3	How about . . . ?	你認為……怎樣（「……」為名詞或動名詞）
4	place (n.)	地方；地點；地區；位置
5	habitat (n.)	棲息地
6	deer (n.)	鹿
7	squirrel (n.)	松鼠
8	rainforest (n.)	熱帶雨林
9	lizard (n.)	蜥蜴
10	crocodile (n.)	鱷魚
11	sand (n.)	沙子
12	rat (n.)	老鼠
13	scorpion (n.)	蠍子
14	spider (n.)	蜘蛛
15	grassland (n.)	草原
16	grass (n.)	草；牧草
17	zebra (n.)	斑馬
18	giraffe (n.)	長頸鹿
19	tundra (n.)	苔原；凍土地帶；凍原
20	caribou (n.)	北美馴鹿

16 Water Habitats

1	cover (v.)	覆蓋
2	include (v.)	包括；包含
3	pond (n.)	池塘
4	salt water	鹹水；海水
5	undersea life	海底生物
6	plankton (n.)	（總稱）浮游生物
7	tiny (a.)	極小的；微小的
8	barely (adv.)	僅僅；勉強；幾乎沒有

9	whale (n.)	鯨魚
10	fresh water	淡水
11	breathe (v.)	呼吸；呼氣；吸氣
12	lungs (n.)	肺；肺臟
13	gill (n.)	（魚）鰓
14	oxygen (n.)	氧氣

17 Weather

1	wake up	醒來；起床
2	weather (n.)	天氣
3	affect (v.)	影響；對……發生作用
4	daily life	日常生活
5	like (prep.)	像；如
6	sunny (a.)	陽光充足的；和煦的；暖和的
7	cloudy (a.)	多雲的；陰天的
8	rainy (a.)	下雨的；多雨的
9	snowy (a.)	雪的；下雪的；多雪的
10	measure (v.)	測量
11	tool (n.)	工具；器具；用具
12	thermometer (n.)	溫度計
13	temperature (n.)	溫度；氣溫
14	unit (n.)	單位；單元
15	degree (n.)	度
16	weather vane	風向計（＝wind vane）
17	indicate (v.)	顯示；指示；指出
18	direction (n.)	方向
19	rain gauge	雨量計
20	find out	找出；發現；查明

18 The Four Seasons

1	season (n.)	季節
2	four seasons	四季
3	change with	隨著……而改變
4	get warmer	變得更暖和
5	rain (v.)	下雨；降雨
6	warmest (a.)	最溫暖的；最暖和的

*原級 – 比較級 – 最高級
  warm（暖和的）– warmer（比較暖和的）– warmest（最暖和的）

7	day (n.)	一天（24小時）；日
8	fall (n.)	秋天（＝autumn）
9	get cooler	變得更涼爽

*原級 – 比較級 – 最高級
  cool（涼快的）– cooler（比較涼快的）– coolest（最涼快的）

10	fall off	從……落下
11	snow (v.)	雪；降雪
12	daylight (n.)	日光；白晝

19 What Can You See in the Sky?

1	clear (a.)	明亮的；晴朗的
2	go outside	到外面
3	look up	向上看；仰視
4	object (n.)	物體
5	night sky	夜空
6	moon (n.)	月亮；月球
7	huge (a.)	龐大的；巨大的
8	ball (n.)	球；球狀體
9	move around	圍繞……運動（＝go around）
10	hundreds of	數以百計；許多
11	tiny (a.)	極小的；微小的
12	gas (n.)	氣體
13	far away	（離……）很遠
14	daytime (n.)	白天；白晝
15	so . . . that . . .	如此……以至於……
16	bright (a.)	明亮的；發亮的；晴朗的
17	still (a.)	靜止的；不動的
18	closest (a.)	最近的

*原級 – 比較級 – 最高級
  close（近的）– closer（比較近的）– closet（最近的）

20 What Causes Day and Night?

1	seem to	看來好像；似乎
2	rise (v.)	（日、月等）上升；升起
3	set (v.)	（日、月等）落；下沈
4	really (adv.)	確實；實際上
5	move (v.)	移動；離開；前進
6	rotate (v.)	旋轉；轉動

7	spin around	（陀螺等）旋轉；（人、物）旋轉
8	like (prep.)	像；如
9	top (n.)	陀螺
10	take (v.)	需要；花費；佔用
11	rotation (n.)	旋轉；（天體）自轉
12	cause (v.)	導致；使發生；引起
13	be shaped	成形；成型；形成
14	face (v.)	面向；正對
15	nighttime (n.)	夜間
16	turn away	轉過去
17	get dark	變暗；變黑
18	repeat (v.)	重複；重做

21　Solids, Liquids, and Gases

1	be made of	由……製成
2	matter (n.)	物質
3	form (n.)	形狀；外形
4	solid (n.)	固體
5	liquid (n.)	液體
6	gas (n.)	氣體
7	touch (v.)	接觸；碰到
8	own (a.)	自己的
9	ice (n.)	冰
10	take (v.)	接受；採取；變成
11	container (n.)	容器
12	coke (n.)	可樂
13	be made up of	由……組成
14	fill (v.)	裝滿；充滿
15	balloon (n.)	氣球
16	steam (n.)	蒸氣；水蒸氣；水氣

22　The Water Cycle

1	change into	改變為……；變化為……
2	water vapor	水蒸氣（＝steam）
3	turn back	變回
4	turn into	變成
5	freeze (v.)	結冰；凝固

6	heat (v.)	把……加熱；變熱；發熱
7	gather (v.)	收集；召集；使聚集
8	cloud (n.)	雲
9	eventually (adv.)	最後；終於
10	release (v.)	釋放；解放
11	fall (v.)	降落；落下

23　Your Body

1	part (n.)	一部分；部分
2	live (v.)	活；活著
3	system (n.)	體系；系統
4	bone (n.)	骨；骨頭
5	hard (a.)	硬的；堅固的
6	inside (prep.)	內部；裡面
7	connect (v.)	連接；連結
8	hold up	托住；支撐
9	protect (v.)	防衛；保護
10	form (v.)	形成；構成；塑造
11	skeletal (a.)	骨骼的
12	skeletal system	骨骼系統
13	muscle (n.)	肌肉
14	laugh (n.)	笑；嘲笑
15	muscular (a.)	肌肉的
16	muscular system	肌肉系統

24　The Systems of Your Body

1	breathe (v.)	呼吸；呼氣；吸氣
2	respiratory (a.)	呼吸的
3	respiratory system	呼吸系統
4	take in	讓……進入；接受
5	move through	通過
6	blood (n.)	血；血液
7	circulate (v.)	（使）循環
8	circulatory (a.)	循環上的
9	circulatory system	血液循環系統
10	be made up of	由……構成
11	heart (n.)	心臟
12	blood vessel	血管

13	**pump** (v.)	把某物從某物抽入、抽出、抽上去
14	**tube** (n.)	管；筒
15	**energy** (n.)	活力；精力
16	**digestive** (a.)	消化的；助消化的
17	**digestive system**	消化系統
18	**break down**	分解

25 **Shapes and Figures**

1	**shape** (n.)	形狀
2	**side** (n.)	邊
3	**triangle** (n.)	三角形
4	**rectangle** (n.)	矩形；長方形
5	**square** (n.)	正方形；方形物；方塊
6	**equal** (a.)	相等的；相當的；均等的
7	**length** (n.)	（距離、尺寸的）長度
8	**circle** (n.)	圓；圓圈
9	**flat** (a.)	平的；平坦的
10	**flat shape**	平面形狀
11	**plane** (n.)	平面
12	**figure** (n.)	圖形
13	**plane figure**	平面圖形
14	**regular** (a.)	規則的；正規的
15	**solid** (n.) (a.)	立體；立體的
16	**solid shape**	立體形狀
17	**sphere** (n.)	球；球體；球形；球面
18	**solid-shaped** (a.)	立體形狀的
19	**cube** (n.)	立方體；立方形物體
20	**cone** (n.)	圓錐體；圓錐形
21	**pyramid** (n.)	三角錐（體）
22	**cylinder** (n.)	圓柱；圓筒；圓柱狀物
23	**solid figure**	立體圖形
24	**look around**	四下觀望；環顧四周

26 **What Am I?**

1	**let** (v.)	讓；允許
2	**myself** (pron.)	我自己
3	**face** (n.)	面

4	**surface** (n.)	面；表面
5	**flat surface**	平面
6	**intersect** (v.)	相交；交叉
7	**various** (a.)	不同的；各種各樣的；形形色色的
8	**point** (n.)	點
9	**edge** (n.)	邊
10	**be formed**	（物體）成形；被形成
11	**vertex** (n.)	頂點
12	**cube** (n.)	立方體；立方形物體

27 **Counting Numbers**

1	**count** (v.)	計算；數
2	**higher than**	比……高
3	**need to**	需要；有……必要
4	**add** (v.)	添加；增加
5	**count by tens**	數十進位；從十數到一百
6	**count backward**	倒數
7	**sometimes** (adv.)	有時；間或
8	**ordinal number**	序數
9	**order** (n.)	順序
10	**position** (n.)	位置；地點；方位
11	**except for**	除了……以外
12	**end in**	以……為結果

28 **Comparing Numbers**

1	**compare** (v.)	比較
2	**value** (n.)	值；數值
3	**example** (n.)	例子；樣本
4	**for example**	例如；舉例來說
5	**number line**	數列
6	**more** (a.)	更多的
7	**greater than**	大於
8	**sign** (n.)	符號
9	**less** (a.)	較小的；較少的
10	**less than**	小於
11	**equal to**	等於
12	**the same as**	與……相同；與……相等

29　Being a Good Writer

1	writer (n.)	作者；作家；記者；撰稿人
2	grammar (n.)	文法
3	punctuation (n.)	標點法；標點
4	language (n.)	語言；語言文字
5	sentence (n.)	句子
6	correct (a.)	正確的；對的
7	expression (n.)	表達；措辭；詞句
8	proper (a.)	適合的；適當的；恰當的
9	punctuation mark	標點符號
10	writing (n.)	書寫；寫作；書面形式
11	capitalization (n.)	大寫
12	capital letter	大寫字母
13	at the beginning of	在……的開頭
14	capitalize (v.)	以大寫字母書寫
15	period (n.)	句號
16	question mark	問號
17	surprise (n.)	驚奇；詫異
18	excitement (n.)	興奮
19	exclamation point	驚嘆號
20	comma (n.)	逗號
21	phrase (n.)	片語；詞組

30　Writing Friendly Letters

1	friendly (a.)	友好的；親切的
2	friendly letter	友善的信
3	Dear (a.)	（信頭稱謂）親愛的；尊敬的
4	stay at	停留在
5	fishing (n.)	釣魚
6	snorkeling (n.)	浮潛
7	summer vacation	暑假
8	be going to	將要……
9	in (prep.)	在……裡；在……上
10	truly (adv.)	真誠地；忠實地
11	greeting (n.)	問候語
12	body (n.)	（文章、書籍等的）正文；主要部分

13	closing (n.)	（演講或書信的）結尾辭
14	forget (v.)	忘記；忽略

31　Aesop's Fables

1	Greek (n.)	希臘人；希臘語
2	slave (n.)	奴隸
3	storyteller (n.)	說故事的人；作家
4	make up	編造；虛構
5	fable (n.)	寓言；虛構的故事；傳說；神話
6	lesson (n.)	教訓；訓誡
7	main (a.)	主要的；最重要的
8	character (n.)	（小說、戲劇等的）人物；角色
9	at the end of	在……的末尾
10	reader (n.)	讀者；愛好閱讀者
11	moral (n.)	（寓言等的）寓意
12	famous (a.)	著名的；出名的
13	ant (n.)	螞蟻
14	grasshopper (n.)	蚱蜢
15	tortoise (n.)	陸龜；龜；烏龜
16	hare (n.)	野兔
17	popular (a.)	廣為流傳的；流行的
18	enjoy (v.)	欣賞；享受；喜愛

32　The Ant and the Grasshopper

1	once (adv.)	昔日；曾經
2	field (n.)	原野；田地；（廣闊的一大片）地
3	gather (v.)	收集；採集
4	play (v.)	玩耍；遊戲；戲弄
5	sing (v.)	歌唱 *動詞三態 sing-sang-sung
6	all . . . long	始終；一整個……
7	even (adv.)	（用於比較級前）甚至更；還
8	still (adv.)	還；仍舊
9	fall (v.)	落下；跌倒 *動詞三態 fall-fell-fallen
10	meal (n.)	膳食；一餐

11	meanwhile (adv.)	其間;同時
12	shiver (v.)	發抖
13	prepare for	為……做準備
14	bad time	倒楣;不愉快的生活;焦慮不安的生活

33 Kinds of Paintings

1	artist (n.)	藝術家;美術家(尤指畫家)
2	create (v.)	創造;創作;設計
3	kind (n.)	種類
4	painting (n.)	繪畫;繪畫藝術;畫法
5	paint (v.)	畫;繪畫
6	landscape (n.)	風景;風景畫
7	scenery (n.)	景色;景物
8	time of the day	一天特定時段
9	still life	靜物畫
10	common (a.)	常見的;一般的
11	work (n.)	著作;作品
12	portrait (n.)	肖像;人像
13	self-portrait (n.)	自畫像
14	himself (pron.)	他自己;他本人

34 Painting and Drawing Materials

1	material (n.)	材料;原料
2	picture (n.)	畫;畫像;圖片;照片
3	drawing (n.)	描繪;素描;圖畫
4	paint (n.)	顏料
5	brush (n.)	毛筆;畫筆
6	canvas (n.)	油畫布;油畫
7	easel (n.)	畫架;黑板架
8	several (a.)	幾個的;數個的
9	oil paint	油畫顏料
10	painter (n.)	畫家
11	produce (v.)	製造;創作
12	rich (a.)	(顏色)濃豔的
13	vivid (a.)	(色彩、光線等)鮮豔的;鮮明的;強烈的
14	prefer (v.)	偏好;更喜歡
15	watercolor (n.)	水彩;水彩顏料

16	finger paint	指畫用的顏料
17	unique (a.)	唯一的;獨一無二的;獨特的
18	brighten (v.)	使明亮;使閃亮
19	crayon (n.)	蠟筆
20	charcoal (n.)	(畫木炭畫的)炭條;炭筆

35 Musical Instruments

1	musical instrument	樂器
2	string (n.)	(樂器等的)弦
3	string instrument	弦樂器
4	bow (n.)	琴弓
5	play (v.)	演奏;彈奏;吹奏
6	pluck (v.)	撥;彈
7	percussion (instrument)	打擊樂器
8	xylophone (n.)	木琴
9	shake (v.)	搖;搖動;震動
10	stick (n.)	木棒
11	woodwind (instrument)	木管樂器
12	blow (v.)	吹奏
13	brass (instrument)	銅管樂器
14	keyboard (instrument)	鍵盤樂器

36 The Orchestra

1	attend (v.)	出席;參加
2	concert (n.)	音樂會;演奏會
3	orchestra (n.)	管弦樂隊
4	make up	組成
5	conductor (n.)	指揮家
6	lead (v.)	領導;指揮;率領
7	stand (v.)	站立;站著
8	in front of	在……的前面
9	conduct (v.)	指揮
10	make sure	設法確保;確定
11	do one's job	做某人的工作
12	at the right time	在正確時刻
13	in harmony	和諧;協調;調和
14	classical music	古典樂
15	opera (n.)	歌劇
16	pop music	流行音樂

Answers and Translations

01 Our Day at School 學校生活

我們每天都去上學。
在學校裡，我們會做各種不同的活動。

每天早上，我們會先向國旗致敬。
我們立正站好，面向國旗。
把右手放在心臟那邊的胸口。
然後誦讀對國家的「效忠誓詞」。

我們在學校裡會學習很多科目。
我們學閱讀和寫字；
我們學做數學題目；
我們學習如何看地圖，認識我們所居住的地球。
在美術課和音樂課上，我們會做很多好玩的活動。

我們和同學一起唸書，一起玩耍。
我們中午會在學校自助餐廳吃飯；
我們會去圖書館借書；
我們會在操場上打球。
我們彼此相處愉快。

* Pledge of Allegiance：（對美國的）效忠誓詞

• **Main Idea and Details**

1 **(a)**   2 **(d)**   3 **(b)**
4 a. **the Pledge of Allegiance**
   b. **We do many fun activities.**   c. **from the library**
5 a. **flag**   b. **solve**   c. **maps**   d. **library**

• **Vocabulary Builder**

1 **activity** 活動   2 **playground**（學校的）操場
3 **classmate** 同班同學   4 **get along** 和睦相處

02 School Rules 學校規則

我們在學校裡要遵守規則。
學校規則規範我們該做什麼，不該做什麼。
有些規則幫助我們與他人和睦相處。
有些規則幫助我們維護自身安全。

在教室裡你應該要遵守規則。
在教室裡保持安靜。
發言前要舉手。
你不該在教室裡大聲叫嚷或奔跑。
你不該打人或跟別人打架。
不要在走廊上奔跑。
打球要到外面的操場。

要聽老師的話，並且服從他們。
要尊敬師長。
老師教育我們，並且幫助我們遵守這些規則。
遵守這些規則能讓學校成為更好的地方。

• **Main Idea and Details**

1 **(b)**   2 **(c)**   3 **(a)**   4 **(d)**
5 a. **quiet**   b. **Raise**   c. **playground**   d. **hallways**

• **Vocabulary Builder**

1 **rule** 規則   2 **follow** 遵守
3 **yell** 叫喊；吼叫   4 **hallway** 走廊

03 Welcome to My Community 歡迎光臨我的社區

我的名字叫做瓊。
我住在一個叫做芝加哥的社區。
社區就是人們共同生活、工作和玩樂的地方。
芝加哥是一個大型城市社區。
許多人在這個社區裡生活和工作。

我家和許多左鄰右舍一起生活。
左鄰右舍們在鄰里間比鄰而居。
我的家和學校都是這個鄰里的一部分；
我們這個鄰里又是社區的一部分。

我的社區裡有許多可供玩樂的地方。
我可以在游泳池裡游泳；
我可以參觀博物館跟欣賞很多有趣的事物；
我可以在中央公園裡野餐和打棒球。
警察局和消防局為這個社區提供服務。
我的社區裡也有很多可以購物的商店。

• **Main Idea and Details**

1 **(c)**   2 **(c)**   3 **(b)**
4 a. **community**   b. **Neighbors**   c. **police station**
5 a. **fun**   b. **neighborhood**   c. **services**   d. **shop**

• **Vocabulary Builder**

1 **community** 社區；共同社會 2 **neighborhood** 鄰近地區；鄰里
3 **museum** 博物館   4 **fire station** 消防局

04 Being a Good Citizen 當一個好公民

每個人都住在一個社區。
住在社區的人必須當一個好公民。
公民是一個社區、州或國家的一分子。

要成為好公民有許多種方式。
好公民尊重他人。
對待別人就像自己希望被對待的樣子。

好公民遵守規則。
我們有必須遵守的規則。
規則可以維持一個社區的清潔和安全。

另一個當好公民的方式是幫助他人。
試著當個好鄰居。
好鄰居會互相幫助和彼此照顧。

- **Main Idea and Details**

1 **(c)**　　2 **(b)**　　3 **(d)**　　4 **(a)**

5 a. **Treat**　　b. **community**　　c. **neighbor**

- **Vocabulary Builder**

1 **citizen** 市民；公民　　2 **state** 州

3 **treat** 對待　　4 **care for** 關心；照顧

Vocabulary Review 1

A　1 **show respect**　　2 **face**
　　3 **right**　　4 **each other**
　　5 **library**　　6 **stay safe**
　　7 **quiet**　　8 **hallways**

B　1 **city**　　2 **neighborhood**
　　3 **police station**　　4 **shopping**
　　5 **ways**　　6 **respects**
　　7 **follows**　　8 **care for**

C　1 **classmate** 同班同學　　2 **playground** 操場；遊樂場
　　3 **community** 社區；共同　　4 **neighbor** 鄰居；鄰近的人
　　　社會　　　　　　　　　　　　（或物）
　　5 **citizen** 市民；公民　　6 **service** 服務

D　1 活動 **d**　　2 面對；面向 **a**
　　3 和睦相處 **b**　　4 教室 **c**
　　5 大叫 **j**　　6 服從；遵守 **f**
　　7 博物館 **h**　　8 服務 **g**
　　9 尊敬 **e**　　10 對待 **i**

05　Celebrating Holidays 慶祝節日

我們每年都會慶祝節日。
節日是一個特別的日子。
每個國家都有一些特別的日子。

在美國，民眾用慶祝節日來紀念重要的人物或事件。
在國定假日，全國都會一起慶祝。
在這些日子我們也會升旗慶祝。

我們在一月慶祝馬丁‧路德‧金恩紀念日。
金恩博士為了非裔美國人的人權努力不懈。
陣亡將士紀念日和退伍軍人節是為了紀念為國家奮鬥的人。
美國獨立紀念日在七月四日。
這天是國家的誕辰。
民眾會舉辦遊行和煙火晚會來慶祝這個日子。
在勞動節，人們會向勞工致敬。

- **Main Idea and Details**

1 **(d)**　　2 **(d)**　　3 **(b)**　　4 **(b)**

5 a. **fought**　　b. **parades**　　c. **working**

- **Vocabulary Builder**

1 **celebrate** 慶祝；過節　　2 **parade** 遊行

3 **veteran** 退役軍人；老兵　　4 **independence** 獨立

06　Holiday Traditions 節日傳統

許多節日都有特殊傳統。
所謂傳統，是長期以來所進行的特殊活動。
傳統年復一年不斷重複進行著。

在母親節，人們會送母親禮物；
在父親節，人們會送父親禮物。
情侶會在情人節互贈禮物。

孩童在萬聖節前夕會穿著嚇人的服裝，
挨家挨戶玩「不給糖就搗蛋」的遊戲。

在中國新年，民眾通常會觀看遊行。
舞龍舞獅是中國新年的一項傳統活動。

在感恩節，家人常會聚在一起。
感恩節吃火雞是一項由來已久的傳統。

在聖誕節，人們會布置聖誕樹。
有些家庭會上教堂做禮拜。
有些家庭會吃聖誕大餐。

* trick-or-treat: trick-or-treat 是萬聖節的主要活動，指萬聖節孩童們挨家挨戶要糖果的遊戲。

* Chinese New Year: 又稱 Lunar New Year（陰曆年，農曆年）。中國的農曆正月初一是春節，又叫陰曆（農曆）年，俗稱「過年」。

- **Main Idea and Details**

1 **(a)**　　2 **(c)**　　3 **(b)**

4 a. **couples**　　b. **They watch parades.**
　c. **on Thanksgiving**

5 a. **Mother's Day**　　b. **Halloween**　　c. **Thanksgiving**

- **Vocabulary Builder**

1 **get together** 聚集　　2 **decorate** 裝飾

3 **dress up** 化裝；打扮　　4 **go to church** 上教堂；做禮拜

07　America's Symbols 美國的象徵

每個國家都有自己的象徵。
所謂象徵，是能代表某種事物的物體。

有許多可代表美國的象徵。
自由鐘意味著自由，
它在西元1776年的7月8日響起，
宣布美國脫離英國獨立。

白頭鷹是美國國鳥，
牠也象徵自由。

自由女神像代表希望和自由。
「自由女神」矗立在紐約港的中央，
對所有來到美國的人表示歡迎。

美國國旗代表美國。
山姆大叔也是美國的象徵。
「山姆大叔」和「美國」的英文縮寫都是「U.S.」，
如同美國國旗一樣，他也穿著紅色、白色和藍色相間的衣服。

• Main Idea and Details

1 **(c)**　　2 **(b)**　　3 **(d)**

4 a. **Liberty Bell**　　b. **Lady Liberty**　　c. **Uncle Sam**

5 a. **freedom**　　b. **Stand for**　　c. **United States**

• Vocabulary Builder

1 **symbol** 符號；象徵

2 **stand for/symbolize** 代表；象徵；意味著

3 **hope** 希望　　4 **welcome** 歡迎

08　National Flags 國旗

每個國家都有國旗，
國旗是一個國家的象徵。

美國國旗被稱為星條旗，
它有13道條紋和50顆星星，
這13道條紋代表美國建國初期的13州；
這50顆星星代表美國目前的50州。
美國國旗的顏色有紅色、白色和藍色。

加拿大是美國北邊的鄰國。
加拿大的國旗由紅色和白色組成，在中間有一個大型的楓葉。
楓樹就是加拿大的國樹。

墨西哥是美國南邊的鄰國。
墨西哥的國旗是綠色、白色和紅色。
在國旗中央，有一隻老鷹站在仙人掌上啄食一條蛇。
這隻老鷹是重要的墨西哥象徵。

• Main Idea and Details

1 **(c)**　　2 **(c)**　　3 **(b)**　　4 **(a)**

5 a. **stripes**　　b. **maple leaf**　　c. **eagle**

• Vocabulary Builder

1 **Stars and Stripes** 星條旗　　2 **Canadian** 加拿大的

3 **represent** 象徵；表示　　4 **current** 現時的；當前的

Vocabulary Review 2

A　1 **celebrate**　　　　2 **national holidays**

　　3 **fly**　　　　　　　4 **Independence**

　　5 **traditions**　　　　6 **Mother's Day**

　　7 **costumes**　　　　8 **Thanksgiving**

B　1 **symbol**　　　　　2 **Liberty Bell**

　　3 **bald eagle**　　　　4 **freedom**

　　5 **national flag**　　　6 **represent**

　　7 **maple leaf**　　　　8 **Mexican**

C　1 **announce** 宣布　　2 **present** 禮物

　　3 **decorate** 裝飾　　4 **symbol** 象徵

　　5 **celebrate** 慶祝　　6 **statue** 雕像；塑像

D　1 慶祝 **i**　　　　　　2 國定假日 **g**

　　3 獨立 **h**　　　　　　4 傳統 **j**

　　5 墨西哥的 **b**　　　　6 裝扮 **d**

　　7 嚇人的 **a**　　　　　8 宣布 **e**

　　9 加拿大的 **f**　　　　10 現時的；當前的 **c**

09　America's Capital 美國的首府

華盛頓 D.C.是美國的首都。
首都是國家重要首長工作的城市。

總統在國家的首都裡生活和工作。
總統領導這個國家。
他和其他政府首長一起工作。

在美國，每個州都有一個首府。
例如，鳳凰城是亞歷桑那州的首府。
檀香山是夏威夷的首府。

州長在州府裡生活和工作。
州長是一個州的領袖。
每個州都有一個州長。
州長和州裡的其他首長一起工作。

• Main Idea and Details

1 **(c)**　　2 **(c)**　　3 **(b)**

4 a. **the city where many important leaders of a country work**
　　b. **the president**　　c. **the leader of a state**

5 a. **President**　　b. **Governor**

• Vocabulary Builder

1 **capital** 首都；首府；國府　　2 **government** 政府

3 **president** 總統　　4 **governor** 州長

10　Washington, D.C. 華盛頓 D.C.

美國最重要的城市之一是華盛頓 D.C.。
為什麼這個城市那麼重要呢？
因為它是國家政府的中心。

白宮位於華盛頓 D.C.。
美國總統在白宮生活和工作。
白宮是國家元首的象徵。

美國國會大廈也在華盛頓 D.C.。
國會大廈是一棟大樓，人們在裡頭開會制定法律。
圓頂風格的建築是國會大廈和每個州議會大廈的象徵。

最高法院也位於華盛頓 D.C.。
法官在法院工作。
法官裁決是否有人違反法律。

華盛頓紀念碑用來紀念喬治・華盛頓。
他是美國第一位總統。

* 華盛頓 D.C. 內的「國會大廈」是「Capitol」；「州議會大廈」是
「capitol」。

• Main Idea and Details

1 **(c)**　　2 **(d)**　　3 **(b)**

4 a. **national**　　b. **Capitol**　　c. **Judges**

5 a. **President**　　b. **laws**　　c. **Judges**　　d. **Washington**

• Vocabulary Builder

1 **dome** 圓屋頂　　　　　　2 **judge** 法官

3 **Capitol** （美國）國會大廈　　4 **monument** 紀念碑

11　Our Land and Water 我們的土地和水源

地球上有許多不同形狀的土地，
這些不同的土地形狀叫作地形。

山是最高的地形。
丘陵沒有山那麼高。
兩座山之間的區域叫做山谷。
森林是被多種樹木所覆蓋的區域。
平原是一片廣大平坦的土地。

被水包圍的地形叫作島嶼。
海洋是面積最大的水。
海洋覆蓋了大部分的地球表面。
湖泊比海洋小。
河川是長條形的水。
河川裡的水通常流入海洋或湖泊。

• Main Idea and Details

1 **(b)**　　2 **(c)**　　3 **(a)**　　4 **(b)**

5 a. **Plain**　　b. **Island**　　c. **Ocean**　　d. **River**

• Vocabulary Builder

1 **landform** 地形　　　　2 **plain** 平原

3 **valley** 山谷　　　　　4 **forest** 森林

12　Where in the World Do We Live?　我們生活在世界何處？

全世界共有七塊大陸。
大陸是一塊很廣大的土地。
你能說出這七塊大陸的名稱嗎？
它們分別是亞洲大陸、非洲大陸、澳洲大陸、歐洲大陸、南極洲大陸、北美洲大陸和南美洲大陸。

亞洲大陸是地球上最大的陸塊；
南極洲大陸是地球上最寒冷的陸塊。
亞洲大陸、非洲大陸和歐洲大陸通常被稱為「舊大陸」；
北美洲大陸和南美洲大陸通常被稱為「新大陸」。

世界上也有五個海洋。
它們分別是太平洋、大西洋、印度洋、南冰洋和北冰洋。
太平洋是最大的海洋。

美國在北美洲大陸；
加拿大在美國北邊；
墨西哥在美國南邊；

大西洋在美國東邊；
太平洋在美國西邊。

你能在地圖上找到你的國家嗎？

• Main Idea and Details

1 **(d)**　　2 **(c)**　　3 **(b)**

4 a. **seven**　　b. **Antarctica**

　　c. **the Pacific, Atlantic, Indian, Antarctic, and Arctic Oceans**

5 a. **South**　　b. **Pacific**　　c. **North America**

• Vocabulary Builder

1 **continent** 大陸；大洲　　2 **be located in** 位於；座落於

3 **Antarctica** 南極洲　　　　4 **next to** 在……旁邊

Vocabulary Review 3

A　1 **Washington, D.C.**　　2 **leads**

　　3 **state capital**　　4 **governor**

　　5 **White House**　　6 **capitol**

　　7 **Court**　　8 **honors**

B　1 **valley**　　2 **surrounded by**

　　3 **Oceans**　　4 **flows into**

　　5 **continents**　　6 **Antarctica**

　　7 **located in**　　8 **next to**

C　1 **capital** 首都；首府；國府　2 **landform** 地形

　　3 **Capitol** （美國）國會大廈　4 **surface** 表面

　　5 **monument** 紀念碑　　6 **continent** 大陸；大洲

D　1 政府 **i**　　2 州長 **a**

　　3 白宮（美國總統官邸）**j**　　4 美國最高法院 **e**

　　5 紀念碑 **h**　　6 地形 **f**

　　7 平原 **b**　　8 位於；座落於 **c**

　　9 太平洋 **g**　　10 舊大陸 **d**

Wrap-Up Test 1

A　1 **get along**　　2 **citizen**

　　3 **celebrate**　　4 **traditions**

　　5 **symbol**　　6 **stands for**

　　7 **national flag**　　8 **continents**

　　9 **Oceans**　　10 **covered**

B　1 市民；公民　　2 州

　　3 關心；照顧　　4 社區；共同社會

　　5 鄰居　　6 規則

　　7 尊敬　　8 走廊

　　9 操場；運動場；遊樂場　　10 旗子

　　11 地圖　　12 同班同學

　　13 遵守　　14 和睦相處

　　15 裝飾　　16 象徵

　　17 代表；象徵；意味著　　18 雕像；塑像

　　19 紀念碑　　20 慶祝；過節

　　21 國定假日　　22 獨立

　　23 特別的　　24 裝扮

　　25 現時的；當前的　　26 地形

13 Parts of Plants 植物的各部位

植物有許多部位。
每個部位都是用來幫助它獲取所需要的養分。

根從土壤中吸收水分和養分，
根也讓植物固定在土中。

莖支撐植物的葉片和花朵，
莖也運送水和養分到植物的其他部位。

葉子替植物製造食物。
葉子利用陽光和空氣來製造食物。

大部分的植物會開花。
花幫助植物繁殖新植物。
花產生種子，然後種子長成新植物。

• **Main Idea and Details**

1 **(b)**　　2 **(a)**　　3 **(b)**

4 a. **soil**　　b. **Leaves**　　c. **Seeds**

5 a. **water**　　b. **nutrients**　　c. **food**　　d. **seeds**

• **Vocabulary Builder**

1 **root** 根　　　　　　　2 **seed** 籽；種子

3 **soil** 土；土壤　　　　4 **grow into** 長成

14 What Do Plants Need? 植物生長需要什麼？

你試過栽種植物嗎？
你或許知道植物的生長需要許多要素。

首先，植物需要水。
植物能夠從土壤或雨中獲得水分。
如果缺水，植物會枯萎。

植物也需要土壤中的養分。
土壤中有許多植物生長所需要的重要養分。

植物也需要空氣和陽光。
葉子幫助植物吸收它所需要的空氣。
葉子也會接收陽光來替植物製造食物。

最後，植物需要空間來成長和保持健康。
當植物逐漸成長茁壯，它們會需要更多生長空間。

• **Main Idea and Details**

1 **(c)**　　2 **(a)**　　3 **(d)**

4 a. **from the ground or from the rain**

　 b. **in the soil**

　 c. **They need more room.**

5 a. **ground**　　b. **soil**　　c. **food**　　d. **grow bigger**

• **Vocabulary Builder**

1 **contain** 包含；容納　　　2 **take in** 吸收；接受

3 **air** 空氣　　　　　　　　4 **healthy** 健康的

15 Where Do Animals Live? 動物在何處生活？

你認為北極熊能夠在沙漠中生活嗎？
魚類呢？

動物在不同的地方生活。
動物生活的地方是牠們的棲息地。
牠們在棲息環境裡能獲得食物和免於威脅。

森林棲地有許多樹木。
鹿、松鼠和兔子這類動物都在森林裡生活；
熱帶雨林幾乎天天下雨，而且整年都很炎熱。
蛇、蜥蜴和鱷魚都在熱帶雨林裡生活；
沙漠非常乾燥，而且有很多沙子。
老鼠、蠍子和蜘蛛這些小動物都在沙漠裡生活；
草原上長滿草。
斑馬、長頸鹿和大象都在草原上生活；
凍原是一個非常寒冷，被白雪覆蓋的地方。
北極熊和北美馴鹿都在凍原上生活。

• **Main Idea and Details**

1 **(c)**　　2 **(b)**　　3 **(c)**　　4 **(b)**

5 a. **rabbits**　　b. **Snakes**　　c. **Polar bears**

• **Vocabulary Builder**

1 **habitat** 棲息地　　　　　2 **caribou** 北美馴鹿

3 **grassland** 草原　　　　　4 **tundra** 苔原；凍土地帶；凍原

16 Water Habitats 水棲地

絕大部分的地球被水覆蓋，
因此地球上有許多水棲地。
包括池塘、湖泊、河川和海洋。

海洋是地球上最大的棲地。
海洋是一大片鹹水。
有很多海底生物生存在海洋裡。
有些動物，像是浮游生物，微小到你根本看不見。
其他像是鯨魚，則是地球上最大的動物。
池塘、湖泊和河川屬於淡水。
也有許多魚類生活在淡水裡。

魚類如何在水中呼吸呢？
陸地上的動物有肺可以呼吸空氣。
而魚類有鰓，
魚類利用鰓來從水中吸取氧氣。

• **Main Idea and Details**

1 **(b)**　　2 **(d)**　　3 **(c)**

4 a. **water**　　b. **Oceans**　　c. **fresh water**

　 d. **Whales**

5 a. **salt**　　b. **fresh**　　c. **gills**

• **Vocabulary Builder**

1 **undersea life** 海底生物　　2 **whale** 鯨魚

3 **plankton** 浮游生物　　　　4 **gills** （魚）鰓

A 1 **absorb** 　　　　2 **support**
　　3 **Leaves** 　　　　4 **grow**
　　5 **contains** 　　　6 **ground**
　　7 **nutrients** 　　　8 **sunlight**

B 1 **habitat** 　　　　2 **forest**
　　3 **desert** 　　　　4 **covered**
　　5 **Oceans** 　　　　6 **Whales**
　　7 **fresh water** 　　8 **oxygen**

C 1 **root**（植物的）根；
　　　　地下莖 　　　2 **stem** 莖；（樹）幹；
　　　　　　　　　　　　　（葉）柄
　　3 **grow** 生長 　　　4 **rainforest**（熱帶）雨林
　　5 **tundra** 苔原；凍土地帶；
　　　　凍原 　　　　6 **undersea life** 海底生物

D 1 營養物 **g** 　　　2 籽；種子 **j**
　　3 土；土壤 **i** 　　4 保持；支撐 **d**
　　5 生長；發育 **a** 　6 吸收；接受 **f**
　　7 健康的 **b** 　　　8 沙漠 **h**
　　9 肺；肺臟 **c** 　　10 鹹水；海水 **e**

17 Weather 天氣

每天，當人們起床時會往外看。
他們在做什麼？
他們在觀察天氣。
天氣對我們的日常生活影響很大。

什麼是天氣？
天氣是外頭的大氣狀態。
天氣可以是晴朗、多雲、下雨或下雪。
它能夠在幾小時內產生變化，或是每天改變。

要如何測量天氣？
我們會利用一些工具去測量天氣。
溫度計測量氣溫。
氣溫能夠顯示空氣有多熱或多冷。
我們測量氣溫的單位叫作「度」。

有些工具用來測量風或雨。
風向計指示風的來向；
雨量計測量下了多少雨。

• **Main Idea and Details**
1 **(b)** 　　2 **(c)** 　　3 **(a)**
4 a. **sunny, cloudy, rainy, and snowy weather**
　　b. **degrees**
　　c. **the direction of the wind**
5 a. **temperature** 　　b. **direction** 　　c. **rain**

• **Vocabulary Builder**
1 **thermometer** 溫度計 　　2 **weather vane** 風向計
3 **measure** 測量 　　　　4 **temperature** 溫度；氣溫

18 The Four Seasons 四季

在許多地方，天氣會隨著季節變化。
一年有四個季節：春天、夏天、秋天和冬天。

春天裡，天氣漸漸變得暖和。
大部分的植物開始生長。
有些地方春天會下很多雨。

夏天的天氣通常很炎熱。
這是一年中最暖和的季節。
夏天的時候，白天很長，所以有日照的時數也很長。

當秋天來臨，天氣漸漸變得涼爽。
葉子開始改變顏色，並且從樹上掉落。

冬天是一年中最寒冷的季節。
有些地方冬天常常下雪。
此外，冬天的白天比較短，
所以有日照的時數也比較短。

• **Main Idea and Details**
1 **(d)** 　　2 **(b)** 　　3 **(b)** 　　4 **(d)**
5 a. **warmer** 　　b. **sunlight** 　　c. **color**

• **Vocabulary Builder**
1 **season** 季節 　　　　2 **day** 白天；白晝
3 **daylight** 日光；白晝 　4 **fall off** 從……落下

19 What Can You See in the Sky? 你能在天空看見什麼？

在晴朗的夜晚，走出戶外，仰望天空，
你或許可以看見許多物體。

夜空中最大的物體是月亮。
月亮是繞著地球運轉的球體巨石。

你還可以看到數以百計的小星星。
事實上，星星是一大團熾熱的氣體。
星星看起來很小，因為它們離地球很遠。
大部分的星星只在夜晚可見。
在白晝，因為陽光很強所以你看不見它們。
但是它們依然在那裡。

白天的時候，你會看見太陽。
你知道太陽也是星體嗎？
太陽看起來這麼亮、這麼大，正因為它是最靠近地球的星體。

• **Main Idea and Details**
1 **(a)** 　　2 **(b)** 　　3 **(a)**
4 a. **moon** 　　b. **tiny** 　　c. **sun**
5 a. **Earth** 　　b. **gases** 　　c. **closest**

• **Vocabulary Builder**
1 **look up** 向上看；仰視 　　2 **bright** 明亮的
3 **tiny** 極小的；微小的 　　4 **far away**（離……）很遠

20 What Causes Day and Night? 白天和黑夜的成因

太陽好像每天早上升起，夜晚落下。
但是太陽並非真的有在移動，而是地球在轉動。

地球會自轉。
自轉就是像陀螺一樣轉動。
地球自轉一次需要24小時。
自轉一次就是一天。

地球的自轉形成了白天和黑夜。
地球的形狀像一顆球。
當地球自轉時，朝向太陽的一面就有陽光。
那一面的地球就是白晝。
另一面就成夜晚。
當地球自轉時，日照的一面會逐漸轉離太陽，漸趨黑暗。
那一面的地球就是夜晚。
原本黑暗的一面進入白天。
這樣的模式每24小時會重複一次。

• **Main Idea and Details**

1 **(c)**   2 **(a)**   3 **(d)**

4 a. **It is shaped like a ball.**   b. **24 hours**
  c. **nighttime**

5 a. **Daytime**   b. **away**

• **Vocabulary Builder**

1 **set**（日、月等）落；下沉   2 **rotate** 旋轉；轉動

3 **shape** 成形   4 **nighttime** 夜晚

Vocabulary Review 5

A 1 **cloudy**   2 **measure**
   3 **degrees**   4 **rain**
   5 **season**   6 **warmest**
   7 **fall off**   8 **daylight**

B 1 **moon**   2 **gases**
   3 **far away**   4 **bright**
   5 **takes**   6 **rotation**
   7 **causes**   8 **rotates**

C 1 **thermometer** 溫度計   2 **daylight** 日光
   3 **rain gauge** 雨量計   4 **tiny** 極小的；微小的
   5 **set**（日、月等）落；下沉   6 **rotate** 旋轉；轉

D 1 顯示；指示；指出 **b**   2 變得更暖和 **f**
   3 變得更涼爽 **e**   4 日光；白晝 **a**
   5 掉落；脫離 **g**   6 向上看；仰視 **h**
   7 物體 **j**   8（離……）很遠 **c**
   9 導致；使發生；引起 **d**   10 重複；重做 **i**

21 Solids, Liquids, and Gases 固體、液體和氣體

世界上每樣東西都由物質組成。
空氣、水和這本書也由物質組成。
物質以三種形態存在，
就是固體、液體和氣體。

固體是摸得到的堅硬物體。
只有固體有屬於自己的形狀。
汽車、書本、石頭和冰塊都是固體。

水是液體。
液體沒有自己的形狀。
裝進什麼容器就是什麼形狀。
果汁、牛奶和可樂都是液體。

空氣由氣體組成。
如同液體一般，氣體沒有自己的形狀。
它會充滿容器內的所有空間。
氣球裡的空氣、氦氣和蒸氣都是氣體。

• **Main Idea and Details**

1 **(b)**   2 **(c)**   3 **(b)**   4 **(a)**

5 a. **shapes**   b. **containers**   c. **steam**

• **Vocabulary Builder**

1 **be made of** 由……製成   2 **solid** 固體

3 **fill** 裝滿；使充滿   4 **gas** 氣體

22 The Water Cycle 水循環

水可以是固體、液體或氣體。
當水遇熱會變成氣體。
這種氣體被稱做水蒸氣。
當水蒸氣冷卻，它會變回水。
當水結冰時，它會變成固態的冰塊。

水的循環導致降雨或降雪。
當海洋和陸地的水經過太陽加熱，
有些水就會變成水蒸氣。
當水蒸氣蒸發到空氣中，
溫度就會降低，
使水蒸氣變回水。

水在天空中以雲的形式聚集，
這些雲最後會釋放出它們的水氣。
天氣溫暖時，這些水會以雨的形式落入地面；
天氣寒冷時，這些水會以雪的形式降落，
然後水循環又重新開始。

• **Main Idea and Details**

1 **(c)**   2 **(a)**   3 **(d)**

4 a. **water vapor**   b. **water**   c. **snow**

5 a. **water vapor**   b. **turns**   c. **rain**

• **Vocabulary Builder**

1 **water vapor** 水蒸氣   2 **water cycle** 水循環

3 **freeze** 結冰；凝固   4 **release** 釋放；解放

23 Your Body 認識你的身體

你的身體有許多不同的部位。
所有部位共同運作協助你維持生命。
現在就讓我們來認識你的身體系統吧。

骨骼是你體內的堅硬部位，
它們負責連接你身體的各個部位。
它們支撐你的身體，形成你的體型。
骨骼也會保護體內許多重要器官。
你的體內共有超過200根骨頭。
它們一起形成你的骨骼系統。

肌肉是能讓你活動的身體組織。
你用肌肉行走、奔跑和跳躍。
你甚至用你的肌肉來說話、飲食、微笑和歌唱。
你的體內有超過600條肌肉。
這些肌群組成你的肌肉系統。

- **Main Idea and Details**

1 **(b)**   2 **(b)**   3 **(c)**
4 a. **more than 200**   b. **more than 600**
    c. **the muscular system**
5 a. **bones**   b. **muscles**   c. **move**

- **Vocabulary Builder**

1 **protect** 防衛；保護   2 **connect** 連接
3 **muscle** 肌肉   4 **jump** 跳；跳躍

24 The Systems of Your Body 認識你的身體系統

讓我們來認識更多你的身體系統吧。

你用你的呼吸系統呼吸，
你的嘴巴和鼻子從空氣中吸入氧氣，
然後，氧氣進入你的肺部，進入血液裡輸送。

你體內的血液經由你的循環系統流動。
循環系統由你的心臟與血管組成。
心臟將血液打入全身的血管。
血管是小的管子，
它們將血液從你的心臟攜帶到身體各個部位。

你的身體從你吃的食物中獲得能量。
當你吃東西時，消化系統會將食物分解，
讓你的身體獲得能量以便工作。

- **Main Idea and Details**

1 **(c)**   2 **(b)**   3 **(a)**   4 **(b)**
5 a. **Takes**   b. **blood vessels**   c. **energy**

- **Vocabulary Builder**

1 **pump** 以幫浦加壓方式輸送   2 **circulate** （使）循環
3 **blood vessel** 血管   4 **digestive system** 消化系統

Vocabulary Review 6

A   1 **matter**   2 **solid**
     3 **shape**   4 **gases**

   5 **changes**   6 **water cycle**
   7 **clouds**   8 **rain**

B   1 **body parts**   2 **connect**
   3 **Muscles**   4 **inside**
   5 **breathe**   6 **circulates**
   7 **made up**   8 **digestive**

C   1 **liquid** 液體   2 **container** 容器
   3 **freeze** 結冰；凝固   4 **skeletal system** 骨骼系統
   5 **muscular system** 肌肉系統
   6 **circulatory system** 血液循環系統

D   1 由……製成 **a**   2 固體 **c**
   3 變回；轉回 **f**   4 變為；使成為 **b**
   5 釋放；解放 **e**   6 防衛；保護 **i**
   7 肌肉 **g**   8 呼吸；呼氣；吸氣 **j**
   9 （使）循環 **d**   10 血管 **h**

Wrap-Up Test 2

A   1 **absorb**   2 **carry**
   3 **habitat**   4 **weather**
   5 **season**   6 **rotation**
   7 **matter**   8 **water cycle**
   9 **muscular**   10 **respiratory**

B   1 （植物的）根；地下莖   2 莖；（樹）幹；（葉）柄
   3 葉子   4 籽；種子
   5 營養物   6 土；土壤
   7 保持；支撐   8 生長；發育；種植
   9 棲息地   10 苔原；凍土地帶；凍原
  11 海底生物   12 （魚）鰓
  13 熱帶雨林   14 鹹水；海水
  15 溫度計   16 圍繞……運動
  17 旋轉；轉動   18 固體
  19 液體   20 水蒸氣
  21 骨骼系統   22 肌肉系統
  23 血液循環系統   24 呼吸系統
  25 消化系統   26 由……製成
  27 變為；使成為   28 釋放；解放
  29 呼吸；呼氣；吸氣   30 （使）循環

25 Shapes and Figures 形狀和圖形

你能說出這些形狀嗎？
有三個邊的形狀叫作三角形。
長方形有四個邊。
正方形有四個相等長度的邊。
圓形是圓的，而且沒有邊。
這些形狀稱為平面形狀，或是平面圖形。
圖形是一個規則形狀。

還有許多立體形狀。
球體是立體的圓；

立方體是立體的正方形。
圓錐體、三角錐體和圓柱體都是立體形狀。
隨處都可見到立體形狀和立體圖形。
它們出現於建築物或是日常用品中。
舉例來說，環顧你的住家或學校，
你看到了什麼圖形呢？

- **Main Idea and Details**

1 **(b)**　　2 **(a)**　　3 **(d)**

4 a. **triangle**　　b. **length**　　c. **solid**　　d. **cube**

5 a. **Triangle**　　b. **Square**　　c. **Sphere**　　d. **cylinders**

- **Vocabulary Builder**

1 **flat shape/plane figure** 平面形狀；平面圖形

2 **solid shape/solid figure** 立體形狀；立體圖形

3 **side** 邊　　4 **rectangle** 長方形

26 What Am I? 我是什麼？

讓我來自我介紹。

我有六個面，
面是立體圖形的平坦表面，
所以我是一個立體圖形。

我的面在不同的點上相交。
當兩個面相交，會形成一個邊。
我有很多邊。
我有十二個邊。

我的面也在不同的頂點處交會。
頂點是指三個或三個以上的邊相交的地方。
我有八個頂點。

現在你知道我是什麼了嗎？
我是一個立方體！

- **Main Idea and Details**

1 **(d)**　　2 **(d)**　　3 **(c)**　　4 **(c)**

5 a. **solid figure**　　b. **faces**　　c. **vertices**

- **Vocabulary Builder**

1 **edge** 邊　　　　　　2 **face** 面

3 **vertex** 頂點　　　　　4 **intersect** 相交；交叉

27 Counting Numbers 1 2 3 數數兒

讓我們從1數到100吧！
一、二、三、四、五，六、七、八、九、十。
那接下來的十個數字呢？
十一、十二、十三、十四、十五，
十六、十七、十八、十九、二十。

我們要如何數大於二十的數兒呢？
首先，我們要先認識這些數字：
三十、四十、五十、六十、七十、八十和九十。
只要在這些數字後面加上1到9的數字就行了，

現在你可以數到100（一百）囉。
讓我們來練習數數看十的倍數：10、20、30、40、50、60、
70、80、90。
接著，練習倒回來數：49、48、47，諸如此類。

我們有時候會使用序數。
我們用序數去描述事物的順序或位置。
前十個序數是第一、第二、第三、第四、第五，
第六、第七、第八、第九和第十。
除了第一、第二和第三之外，其他序數都以「th」結尾。

- **Main Idea and Details**

1 **(c)**　　2 **(c)**　　3 **(a)**　　4 **(d)**

5 a. **twelve**　　b. **thirty-two**　　c. **forty-five**
　　d. **third**　　e. **ninth**

- **Vocabulary Builder**

1 **count backward** 倒數

2 **count by tens** 數十進位；從十數到一百

3 **add** 加上　　4 **ordinal number** 序數

28 Comparing Numbers 數字大小比一比

讓我們來比較數值。

在一條數列上，某個數字一定比前一個數字多 1。
舉例來說，6 比 5 多 1，
所以我們可以說「6 比 5 大」，
或者我們也可以寫成：6 > 5。
「>」這個符號代表「大於」。

在一條數列上，某個數字一定比下一個數字少 1。
舉例來說，3 比 4 少 1，
所以我們可以說「3 小於 4」或是 3 < 4。
「<」這個符號代表「小於」。

有時候，兩個數字有相等的值。
舉例來說，「3 等於 3」。
我們也可以寫成：3 = 3。
「=」這個符號代表「等於」或「與……相同」。

- **Main Idea and Details**

1 **(a)**　　2 **(b)**　　3 **(a)**

4 a. **less**　　b. **more**　　c. **is greater**　　d. **is less**

5 a. **after**　　b. **before**　　c. **same**

- **Vocabulary Builder**

1 **compare** 比較　　　　　2 **value** 值；數值

3 **equal to** 等於　　　　　4 **number line** 數列

Vocabulary Review 7

A　1 **triangle**　　　　　2 **figure**
　　　3 **sphere**　　　　　4 **solid**
　　　5 **flat surface**　　　6 **intersect**
　　　7 **edge**　　　　　　8 **vertex**

B　1 **count**　　　　　　2 **by tens**
　　　3 **backward**　　　　4 **ordinal numbers**

5 after	6 greater
7 less	8 equal

C 1 **triangle** 三角形　　2 **edge** 邊
　　3 **pyramid** 三角錐；金字塔　4 **vertex** 頂點
　　5 **ordinal number** 序數　6 **number line** 數列

D 1 立體形狀 **g**　　　　2 邊 **c**
　　3 矩形；長方形 **d**　　4 平面 **f**
　　5 倒數 **e**　　　　　6 順序 **i**
　　7 正方形；方形物；方塊 **a**　8 值；數值 **b**
　　9 符號 **h**　　　　　10 比較 **j**

29 Being a Good Writer 當一個優秀作家

一個優秀作家會使用正確的文法和標點符號。
文法是一個語言的規則。
當你寫一個句子，要使用正確的文字和用語。
同時，使用適當的標點符號去標示句子該在何處停止。

這裡有一些寫作規則。

大寫使用規則：
1. 句首字母要大寫。
2. 「I」這個字一律大寫。
3. 人名或特定地名的字首要大寫。
4. 星期、月分和節日名的字首要大寫。

標點符號使用規則：
1. 句子的結尾要加句號。
2. 問句要加問號。
3. 使用驚嘆號表達驚訝或興奮。
4. 在一系列人名、地點、物品或片語之間使用逗號。

• **Main Idea and Details**
1 **(a)**　　2 **(c)**　　3 **(d)**
4 a. **capitalize**　　b. **period**　　c. **exclamation point**
5 a. **sentence**　　b. **months**　　c. **period**
　 d. **exclamation**

• **Vocabulary Builder**
1 **capitalize** 以大寫字母寫　2 **grammar** 文法
3 **punctuation** 標點法；標點符號　4 **exclamation point** 驚嘆號

30 Writing Friendly Letters 書寫友善的信

2017年8月5日

親愛的莎拉：

你好嗎？
我最近很好。

我和家人度過了一個很棒的暑假。
我們在棕櫚灘待了一星期。
我有去游泳和釣魚。
有一天我們甚至跑去浮潛！

你的暑假過得如何呢？
再過兩個星期就要開學了，
到時候課堂上見。

湯姆
敬上

1 **日期**：在頂端寫下日期，月分的字首要大寫。寫日期的時候，
　日和年之間要加逗號。
2 **問候語**：用Dear開頭，後面加上朋友的名字。字首字母要大
　寫，並在問候語後面加上逗號。
3 **內文**：信件內文是你所要傳達的訊息，每個句子的第一個字母
　要大寫。
4 **結語**：用結語和你的名字做結尾，結語後面要放逗號。別忘了
　結語和你的名字的字首要大寫。
*大寫：人名和特殊地名的首字母要大寫。
*標點符號：使用適當的標點符號，檢查信中的句號、逗號、問號
　　　　　和驚嘆號是否都正確。

• **Main Idea and Details**
1 **(b)**　　2 **(b)**　　3 **(a)**
4 a. **a comma**　　b. **with "Dear"**　　c. **with a capital letter**
5 a. **year**　　b. **Dear**　　c. **closing**

• **Vocabulary Builder**
1 **friendly** 友好的；親切的　2 **greeting** 問候語
3 **closing** 結語　　4 **body** 內文；正文

31 Aesop's Fables 伊索寓言

很久以前，有一個男人住在希臘的薩默斯島。
他的名字叫伊索，他是一個奴隸。
但他也是一個偉大的說故事家。
伊索常常編故事給人們聽。

他的故事被稱為寓言。
寓言是富有教育意義的短篇故事。
伊索寓言的主角通常是動物。
這些動物像人一樣說話行動。
在寓言的最後，伊索總是告訴讀者一個箴言。
這些箴言就是故事的寓意。

伊索寫了許多著名的寓言故事，
〈螞蟻與蚱蜢〉就是其中之一，

〈龜兔賽跑〉也非常知名。
如今，不論老老少少都喜歡閱讀伊索寓言。

• Main Idea and Details

1 **(c)**　　2 **(c)**　　3 **(b)**　　4 **(c)**

5 a. **Greek**　　b. **stories**　　c. **moral**　　d. **Ant**

• Vocabulary Builder

1 **fable** 寓言　2 **storyteller** 說故事的人；作家

3 **character**（小說、戲劇等的）人物；角色

4 **moral**（寓言等的）寓意

32 The Ant and the Grasshopper 螞蟻和蚱蜢

從前，有一隻螞蟻和蚱蜢住在同一片原野上。
螞蟻每天辛勤工作，收集食物準備過冬。
但是蚱蜢整個夏天都在玩樂和歌唱。

夏天過去秋天來臨，天氣開始變冷。
螞蟻比之前更賣力工作，
但是蚱蜢仍舊繼續玩樂。

有一天，降下初雪。
螞蟻躲進洞內，飽餐一頓。
這時，蚱蜢開始在寒風中顫抖。
他說道：「我又冷又餓，該怎麼辦？」

當春天來臨，天氣轉為暖和。
螞蟻走出戶外，
卻再也沒有看見蚱蜢了。

寓意：在好日子裡別忘記為壞日子作準備。

• Main Idea and Details

1 **(b)**　　2 **(a)**　　3 **(a)**

4 a. **hard**　　b. **sang**　　c. **winter**

5 a. **food**　　b. **meals**　　c. **Shivered**　　d. **hungry**

• Vocabulary Builder

1 **gather** 收集；採集　　　　2 **field** 原野；田野

3 **shiver** 發抖　　　　　　　4 **grasshopper** 蚱蜢

Vocabulary Review 8

A　1 grammar　　　　　　2 sentence
　　3 Capitalize　　　　　4 period
　　5 proper　　　　　　　6 greetings
　　7 body　　　　　　　　8 vacation

B　1 made up　　　　　　2 famous
　　3 fable　　　　　　　4 moral
　　5 grasshopper　　　　6 harder
　　7 shivering　　　　　8 prepare for

C　1 gather 收集；採集　　2 snorkeling 浮潛
　　3 punctuation mark 標點符號　4 fable 寓言
　　5 character（小說、戲劇等的）人物；角色
　　6 meal 膳食；一餐

D　1 以大寫字母寫 **b**　　　　2 大寫 **d**
　　3 興奮 **e**　　　　　　　　4 友好的；親切的 **c**
　　5 奴隸 **f**　　　　　　　　6 說故事的人；作家 **h**
　　7 道德；（寓言等的）寓意 **j**　8 收集；採集 **i**
　　9 準備 **g**　　　　　　　　10 發抖 **a**

33 Kinds of Paintings 繪畫的種類

畫家們創作許多種類的繪畫。

有些藝術家喜愛風景畫。
風景畫最重要的元素就是景物。
景物通常包括土地、樹木、天空、湖泊和河川。
天氣、季節和一日當中的時段也很重要。

有些藝術家喜愛靜物畫。
靜物畫裡的物體不會移動，
因此被稱做靜物畫。
要畫靜物畫，畫家必須先準備要畫的物體。
靜物畫通常包括水果、花卉和其他小型物品。

人物畫是其他常見的繪畫作品。
人物畫叫作肖像。
自畫像是畫家自己的肖像。

• Main Idea and Details

1 **(d)**　　2 **(b)**　　3 **(b)**　　4 **(c)**

5 a. **scenery**　　b. **objects**　　c. **person**

• Vocabulary Builder

1 **landscape** 風景畫　　　　2 **artist** 藝術家；畫家

3 **still life** 靜物畫　　　　4 **self-portrait** 自畫像

34 Painting and Drawing Materials 繪畫和繪畫材料

畫家需要特殊的材料去製作他們的圖畫。
他們需要繪畫材料、顏料、畫筆、畫布和畫架。

繪畫顏料的種類非常多。
許多畫家喜愛油性顏料。
油性顏料能為圖畫營造出濃厚且鮮豔的顏色效果。
其他畫家偏愛使用水彩和指畫用顏料。
水彩畫通常非常明亮。
指畫用顏料能創作出獨特且趣味的圖畫。

繪畫材料也有各式各樣的選擇。
當然，有些畫家只使用簡單的鉛筆。
其他人會使用彩色鉛筆讓畫作更明亮。
有些人偏好五顏六色的蠟筆。
有些畫家則用炭筆畫畫。
所有的繪畫材料都能創造出偉大的畫作。

• Main Idea and Details

1 **(c)**　　2 **(c)**　　3 **(b)**

4 a. **materials**　　b. **finger**　　c. **colors**

5 a. **Watercolors**　　b. **Color pencils**

1 **painter** 畫家　　　　2 **easel** 畫架

3 **vivid** 色彩鮮豔的　　　4 **drawing materials** 繪畫材料

35　Musical Instruments 認識樂器

樂器的種類林林總總。

讓我們先來認識一下弦樂家族。
你能說出幾個有弦的樂器嗎？
小提琴？大提琴？還是吉他呢？
你通常用弓去演奏弦樂器，
但是有時可以用手指撥弦。

接著讓我們來介紹打擊樂器。
打擊樂器包括鼓、木琴和鈴鼓。
打擊樂器很有趣。
你可以用手或棒子去敲打或搖動它們。

木管樂器是另一種常見樂器。
木管樂器有單簧管、長笛和雙簧管。
音樂家藉由吹入空氣來演奏木管樂器。
音樂家也會吹奏銅管樂器。
小號和長號都屬於銅管樂器。

鋼琴和風琴屬於鍵盤樂器。
你能用手指彈奏鍵盤樂器。

• Main Idea and Details

1 (c)　　　2 (c)　　　3 (a)

4 a. **string**　　b. **percussion**　　c. **blow**

5 a. **bow**　　b. **shake**　　c. **Blow**　　d. **Piano**

• Vocabulary Builder

1 **musical instrument** 樂器

2 **percussion (instruments)** 打擊樂器

3 **musician** 音樂家

4 **keyboard (instruments)** 鍵盤樂器

36　The Orchestra 管弦樂隊

你曾經參加過演奏會嗎？
你曾經在電視上看過管弦樂隊嗎？
所有的樂器都會出現在管弦樂隊裡。
管弦樂隊由弦樂器、打擊樂器、木管樂器、銅管樂器和鍵盤樂器所組成。
音樂家們齊聚一堂，演奏出美妙的音樂。

指揮家負責領導管弦樂隊。
他或她站在管弦樂隊前方，指揮音樂演出。
指揮家確保所有演奏者能在正確的時間演奏他們負責的樂器。
讓他們能奏出和諧的曲調。

大部分的管弦樂隊演奏古典樂。
他們可能會演奏莫札特或巴哈的音樂。
但是有的管弦樂隊也會演奏歌劇或流行音樂。

• Main Idea and Details

1 (b)　　　2 (d)　　　3 (a)

4 a. **string**, **percussion**, **woodwind**, **brass**, and **keyboard instruments**　　b. **the conductor**
　c. **classical music**

5 a. **woodwind**　　b. **harmony**　　c. **classical**

• Vocabulary Builder

1 **orchestra** 管弦樂隊　　　2 **classical music** 古典音樂

3 **conductor** 指揮家　　　4 **opera** 歌劇

Vocabulary Review 9

A　1 **paintings**　　　　2 **scenery**
　　3 **still life**　　　　4 **self-portrait**
　　5 **materials**　　　　6 **Oil paints**
　　7 **Watercolor**　　　　8 **drawing**

B　1 **instruments**　　　　2 **string**
　　3 **blowing**　　　　4 **woodwinds**
　　5 **attended**　　　　6 **orchestra**
　　7 **leads**　　　　8 **classical**

C　1 **watercolor** 水彩　　　2 **scenery** 景色；景物
　　3 **still life** 靜物畫　　　4 **concert** 音樂會；演奏會
　　5 **string (instruments)** 弦樂器　　6 **conductor** 指揮家

D　1 畫家 **i**　　　　2 流行的；受歡迎的 **c**
　　3 偏好；更喜歡 **d**　　　4 繪畫材料 **b**
　　5 打擊樂器 **j**　　　　6 樂器 **f**
　　7 銅管樂器 **g**　　　　8 管弦樂隊 **h**
　　9 出席；參加 **e**　　　　10 指揮 **a**

Wrap-Up Test 3

A　1 **flat shapes**　　　　2 **solid shapes**
　　3 **greater**　　　　4 **the same**
　　5 **grammar**　　　　6 **Capitalize**
　　7 **fables**　　　　8 **bad times**
　　9 **musical**　　　　10 **Oil paints**

B　1 平面圖形　　　　2 立體圖形
　　3 邊　　　　4 面
　　5 頂點　　　　6 長方形
　　7 圓錐體　　　　8 球體
　　9 序數　　　　10 數列
　　11 以大寫字母書寫　　12 大寫
　　13 大寫字母　　　　14 標點符號
　　15 友好的；親切的　　16 寓言
　　17（小說、戲劇等的）人物；角色　18 膳食；一餐
　　19（寓言等的）寓意　　20 蚱蜢
　　21 肖像；人像　　　　22 風景；風景畫
　　23 靜物畫　　　　24 顏料
　　25 繪畫材料　　　　26 偏好；更喜歡
　　27 獨特的　　　　28 打擊樂器
　　29 木管樂器　　　　30 銅管樂器

FUN學 美國英語閱讀課本 1
各學科實用課文

Authors

Michael A. Putlack
Michael A. Putlack graduated from Tufts University in Medford, Massachusetts, USA, where he got his B.A. in History and English and his M.A. in History. He has written a number of books for children, teenagers, and adults.

e-Creative Contents
A creative group that develops English contents and products for ESL and EFL students.

作者	Michael A. Putlack & e-Creative Contents
翻譯	丁宥暄
編輯	丁宥榆／丁宥暄
製程管理	洪巧玲
發行人	黃朝萍
出版者	寂天文化事業股份有限公司
電話	+886-(0)2-2365-9739
傳真	+886-(0)2-2365-9835
網址	www.icosmos.com.tw
讀者服務	onlineservice@icosmos.com.tw
出版日期	2024 年 07 月 二版再刷 (寂天雲隨身聽 APP 版) (0207)

國家圖書館出版品預行編目 (CIP) 資料

FUN 學美國英語閱讀課本 : 各學科實用課文 (寂天雲隨身聽
APP 版) / Michael A. Putlack, e-Creative Contents 著 ; 丁宥暄
譯 . -- 二版 . -- [臺北市] : 寂天文化 , 2021.02- 印刷
冊 ;　公分

ISBN 978-986-318-981-7(第 1 冊 : 菊 8K 平裝)

1. 英語　2. 讀本

805.18　　　　　　　　　　　110001845

FÜN學

美國英語閱讀課本

各學科實用課文 二版

1

Workbook

AMERICAN
SCHOOL
TEXTBOOK

READING KEY

作者 Michael A. Putlack & e-Creative Contents　譯者 丁宥暄

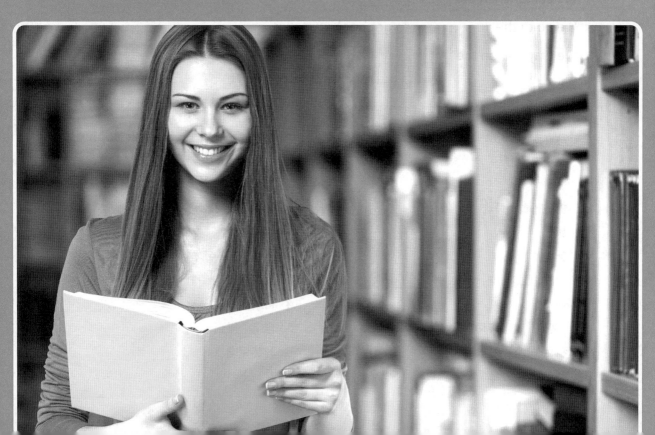

🎧 37

A Listen to the passage and fill in the blanks.

We go to _____ each day.

At school, we do many different _____ .

Every morning, we show _____ to the flag.

We stand up and face the _____ .

We put our _____ hand over our heart.

And we say the Pledge of Allegiance.

We learn many _____ at school.

We learn _____ _____ read and write.

We learn how to _____ math problems.

We read _____ and learn about the world we live in.

In art and music _____ , we do many fun activities.

We study together and play together with our _____ .

We eat lunch in the _____ .

We go to the _____ to get books.

We play ball on the _____ .

We _____ _____ with each other.

B Write the meaning of each word or phrase from Word List (main book p.104) in English.

1	活動	_____	9	（指方式、方法）怎樣；怎麼	_____
2	對……表示尊敬	_____	10	解答（數學題）	_____
3	旗子	_____	11	數學題	_____
4	起立	_____	12	班級；（一節）課；上課	_____
5	面對；面向	_____	13	同班同學	_____
6	放；擺	_____	14	自助餐廳	_____
7	（美國）效忠國家的宣誓	_____	15	獲得；得到	_____
8	科目；學科	_____	16	和睦相處	_____

Daily Test 02 School Rules

A Listen to the passage and fill in the blanks. 🎧 38

We have _____ to follow at school.

Rules tell us _____ to do and what not to do.

Some rules help us get along with _____ _____.

Some rules help us stay _____.

You should _____ the rules in your classroom.

Be quiet in the _____.

_____ your hand before speaking.

You should not _____ or run in the classroom.

You should not hit or _____ each other.

Do not run in the _____.

Play ball _____ on the playground.

Listen to your teachers and _____ them.

Show respect to your _____.

Teachers teach us and _____ us follow the rules.

Following the rules makes the school a _____ place.

B Write the meaning of each word or phrase from Word List in English.

1 規則 _____
2 遵守 _____
3 彼此；互相 _____
4 繼續；保持 _____
5 安全的 _____
6 教室 _____
7 安靜的 _____
8 舉起；抬起 _____
9 叫喊；吼叫 _____
10 打架；爭吵 _____
11 互相 _____
12 走廊 _____
13 在外面 _____
14 運動場；操場；遊樂場 _____
15 服從；遵守 _____
16 更好的 _____

A Listen to the passage and fill in the blanks.

🎧 39

My name is June.

I live in a _____ called Chicago.

A community is a place where people live, work, and have fun _____.

Chicago is a big _____ community.

Many people live and _____ in my community.

My family lives with many _____.

Neighbors live _____ together in a neighborhood.

My home and school are part of my _____.

And my neighborhood is _____ of my community.

There are many places to have _____ in my community.

I can swim in the _____.

I can visit the _____ and see many interesting things.

In Central Park, I can have a _____ and play baseball.

The police station and _____ _____ provide services for the community.

My community has many _____ for shopping, too.

B Write the meaning of each word or phrase from Word List in English.

1 社區；共同社會 _____
2 娛樂；樂趣 _____
3 與……住在一起 _____
4 鄰居；鄰近的人(或物) _____
5 近鄰；鄰近地區；整個街坊 _____
6 一部分；部分 _____
7 游泳池 _____

8 博物館 _____
9 去野餐；舉行野餐 _____
10 打棒球 _____
11 警察局 _____
12 消防局 _____
13 提供 _____
14 服務 _____

04 Being a Good Citizen

A Listen to the passage and fill in the blanks. 🎧 40

Everyone lives _____ a community.

People in communities need to be good _____.

A citizen is a _____ of a community, state, or country.

There are many _____ to be a good citizen.

A good citizen _____ others.

Treat others as you would like to be _____.

A good citizen follows _____.

We have rules that we _____ all follow.

Rules _____ a community clean and safe.

Another way to be a good citizen is to _____ others.

Try to be a good _____.

Good neighbors help each other and _____ _____ one another.

B Write the meaning of each word or phrase from Word List in English.

1	住在…… _____	8	尊敬 _____
2	需要；必要 _____	9	其它的人（或物）_____
3	市民；公民 _____	10	對待 _____
4	成員 _____	11	想要…… _____
5	（美國的）州 _____	12	被對待 _____
6	國家；國土 _____	13	持有；保有 _____
7	路；方法；方式 _____	14	關心；照顧 _____

A Listen to the passage and fill in the blanks. 🎧 41

> We _____ holidays every year.
>
> A _____ is a special day.
>
> Every country has some _____ days.
>
> In the U.S., people celebrate holidays to _____ important people or events.
>
> On _____ holidays, the whole country celebrates together.
>
> We also _____ the flag on these days.
>
> Martin Luther King, Jr. Day is celebrated _____ January.
>
> Dr. King worked hard _____ African-Americans.
>
> Memorial Day and Veterans Day honor the people who _____ for the country.
>
> Independence Day is celebrated _____ the 4th of July.
>
> It is the country's _____.
>
> People celebrate that day with _____ and fireworks.
>
> On Labor Day, people show respect for _____ people.

B Write the meaning of each word or phrase from Word List in English.

1 慶祝；過節 _____
2 節日；假日 _____
3 特別的 _____
4 尊敬；敬重；給予（某人）以……的榮譽 _____
5 事件；大事 _____
6 國定假日 _____
7 懸掛（旗）；升（旗）_____
8 馬丁・路德・金恩紀念日 _____
9 被慶祝 _____
10 非裔美國人 _____
11 （美國）陣亡將士紀念日 _____
12 （美國）退伍軍人節 _____
13 獨立 _____
14 （美國）獨立紀念日 _____
15 煙火；放煙火；煙火大會 _____
16 （美國）勞動節 _____

06 Holiday Traditions

A Listen to the passage and fill in the blanks. 🎧 42

Many holidays have special _____.

A tradition is a special way that something has been done for

a _____ _____.

Traditions are _____ year after year.

On Mother's Day, people give _____ to their mothers.

On _____ Day, people give presents to their fathers.

Couples give each other _____ on Valentine's Day.

Children dress up in scary _____ on Halloween.

Then they go trick-or-treating for _____.

On Chinese New Year, people usually watch _____.

The _____ parade is a tradition on this holiday.

Families often _____ _____ on Thanksgiving.

It's an old tradition to eat _____ on Thanksgiving.

On Christmas, people _____ a Christmas tree.

Some families go to _____.

Some families have a big holiday _____.

B Write the meaning of each word or phrase from Word List in English.

1 傳統 _____

2 重複；重做 _____

3 每年；年復一年 _____

4 母親節 _____

5 禮物 _____

6 情人節 _____

7 裝扮 _____

8 嚇人的 _____

9 （特定場合之）服裝；裝束 _____

10 萬聖節前夕（10月31日） _____

11 不給糖就搗蛋 _____

12 中國新年；春節；農曆新年 _____

13 聚集；聚會 _____

14 感恩節 _____

15 裝飾 _____

16 晚餐；晚宴 _____

07 America's Symbols

A Listen to the passage and fill in the blanks. 🎧43

Every country has its own _____.

A symbol is an object that _____ _____ something else.

There are many _____ symbols.

The Liberty Bell stands for _____.

The Liberty Bell was _____ on July 8, 1776.

It _____ America's freedom from England.

The bald _____ is the national bird.

It also _____ freedom.

The Statue of Liberty stands for _____ and freedom.

"Lady Liberty" _____ in the middle of New York Harbor.

She _____ all people to the country.

The American _____ stands for the United States.

_____ Sam is a symbol of the United States, too.

"Uncle Sam" and "United States" both start with the _____ "U.S."

He also wears red, white, and blue _____ like the American flag.

B Write the meaning of each word or phrase from Word List in English.

1 符號；象徵　_____

2 物體　_____

3 代表；象徵；意味著 _____

4 自由鐘　_____

5 自由；獨立自主 _____

6 按鈴；搖鈴；敲鐘 _____

7 宣布；發布 _____

8 白頭鷹　_____

9 象徵；標誌　_____

10 自由女神像　_____

11 雕像；塑像　_____

12 站立；立定　_____

13 在……中間；在……中途 _____

14 紐約港　_____

15 歡迎；接待　_____

16 山姆大叔（美國政府的綽號）_____

A Listen to the passage and fill in the blanks. ∩44

Every country has a _____ flag.

A national flag is a symbol that stands for a _____.

The American flag is called the Stars and _____.

The flag has 13 stripes and _____ stars.

The 13 stripes _____ the first 13 states of the U.S.

The 50 stars represent the _____ 50 states of the U.S.

The flag's _____ are red, white, and blue.

Canada is America's _____ neighbor.

The Canadian flag is red and white and has a big _____ _____ in the middle.

The maple is _____ national tree.

Mexico is America's _____ neighbor.

The _____ flag is green, white, and red.

In the center, there is an eagle eating a snake on a _____.

The _____ is an important Mexican symbol.

B Write the meaning of each word or phrase from Word List in English.

1 全國性的；國家的 _____

2 國旗 _____

3 美國的 _____

4 星條旗 _____

5 條紋；線條 _____

6 象徵；表示 _____

7 現時的；當前的 _____

8 （在）北方的；向北方的；來自北方的
_____

9 加拿大的 _____

10 楓葉 _____

11 楓樹 _____

12 （在）南方的；向南方的 _____

13 墨西哥的 _____

14 老鷹 _____

15 蛇 _____

16 仙人掌 _____

A Listen to the passage and fill in the blanks. 🎧 45

Washington, D.C. is the _____ of the United States.

A capital is the city where many important _____ of a country work.

The _____ lives and works in the country's capital.

The president _____ the country.

He works with other _____ leaders.

In the U.S., each _____ has a capital, too.

For example, Phoenix is the capital city of _____.

_____ is the capital city of Hawaii.

The _____ lives and works in the state capital.

The governor is the _____ of the state.

_____ state has a governor.

The governor _____ with other state leaders.

B Write the meaning of each word or phrase from Word List in English.

1 首都；首府   _____
2 領袖；領導者   _____
3 總統   _____
4 領導；指揮；率領 _____
5 與……共事；與……協作 _____
6 政府   _____

7 州   _____
8 國府；州府   _____
9 美國亞利桑那州 _____
10 美國夏威夷州   _____
11 州長   _____
12 州府   _____

10 Washington, D.C.

A Listen to the passage and fill in the blanks. 🎧46

One of the most important cities in the U.S. is _____, D.C.

Why is it so important?

Because it is the _____ of the national government.

The _____ _____ is in Washington, D.C.

The _____ of the United States lives and works in the White House.

The White House is a _____ of the nation's leader.

The _____ is there, too.

A capitol is a building where people meet to make _____.

The _____ style is also a symbol of the capitol buildings in each state.

The Supreme _____ is also there.

_____ work in a court.

Judges decide if laws have been _____.

The Washington _____ honors George Washington.

He was the _____ president of the United States.

B Write the meaning of each word or phrase from Word List in English.

1 （尤指非常時期成立的）聯合政府；國民聯合政府

_____

2 白宮（美國總統官邸） _____

3 （美國）國會大廈 _____

4 制定法律 _____

5 圓屋頂；圓蓋 _____

6 風格；作風；樣式；類型 _____

7 （美國）州議會大廈 _____

8 最高法院 _____

9 法官；裁判 _____

10 法庭；法院 _____

11 決定；裁決；判決 _____

12 被打破；被違反；被損壞 _____

13 華盛頓紀念碑 _____

14 紀念碑；紀念塔；紀念館 _____

A Listen to the passage and fill in the blanks. 🎧 47

The earth has many different _____ of land.

These different shapes are called _____.

A _____ is the highest form of land.

A _____ is not as high as a mountain.

We call the area between two mountains a _____.

A forest is an area _____ with many kinds of trees.

A plain is a large, _____ land.

A landform that is _____ by water is called an island.

An _____ is the largest body of water.

Oceans cover most of the earth's _____.

A _____ is smaller than an ocean.

A _____ is a long body of water.

The water in a river usually _____ into the ocean or a lake.

B Write the meaning of each word or phrase from Word List in English.

1 形狀；外形 _____
2 陸地；土地 _____
3 被叫做；被視為…… _____
4 地形 _____
5 形狀；外形；種類；類型 _____
6 像……一樣高；像……那麼高 _____
7 山谷；溪谷 _____
8 被……覆蓋 _____
9 種類；性質 _____
10 平地；平原；曠野 _____
11 平的；平坦的 _____
12 被……包圍；被……環繞 _____
13 海洋；海 _____
14 島 _____
15 表面 _____
16 流入 _____

12 Where in the World Do We Live?

The world has _____ continents.

A _____ is a very large piece of land.

Can you _____ the seven continents?

They are Asia, Africa, Australia, _____, Antarctica, and North and South America.

Asia is the _____ continent on Earth.

_____ is the coldest continent on Earth.

Asia, Africa, and Europe are often called the "_____ _____."

North and South America are _____ called "the New World."

The world has five _____, too.

They are the _____, Atlantic, Indian, Antarctic, and Arctic oceans.

The Pacific is the _____.

The United States is _____ in North America.

Canada is _____ to the U.S. to the north.

Mexico is next to the U.S. to the _____.

The _____ Ocean is to the east of the U.S.

The Pacific Ocean is to the _____ of the U.S.

Can you find _____ your country is on a map?

1	大陸；大洲	_____	11	地球上；世界上 _____
2	一個；一張；一片；一塊	_____	12	最冷的；最寒冷的 _____
3	列舉；陳說；說出……的名字	_____	13	舊大陸 _____
4	亞洲	_____	14	新大陸 _____
5	非洲	_____	15	太平洋 _____
6	澳洲	_____	16	大西洋 _____
7	歐洲	_____	17	印度洋 _____
8	南極洲	_____	18	北冰洋 _____
9	北美洲	_____	19	位於；座落於 _____
10	最大的；最廣泛的	_____	20	緊鄰著 _____

13 Parts of Plants

A Listen to the passage and fill in the blanks. 🎧49

Plants have many _____.

Each part of a plant helps the plant get what it _____.

Roots _____ water and nutrients from the soil.

The _____ also hold the plant in the ground.

Stems _____ the plant's leaves and flowers.

The stems also _____ water and nutrients to other plant parts.

Leaves make _____ for the plant.

_____ use sunlight and air to make the food.

Most plants also have _____.

Flowers help plants make new _____.

The flowers make seeds, and then the _____ grow into new plants.

B Write the meaning of each word or phrase from Word List in English.

1 部位；部分　　_____

2 需要；有……必要　_____

3 吸收（液體、氣體、光、聲等）_____

4 營養物　_____

5 土；土壤　_____

6 （植物的）根；地下莖 _____

7 保持；支撐　_____

8 土壤；土地；地面　_____

9 莖；（樹）幹；（葉）柄 _____

10 支撐　_____

11 葉子　_____

12 花　_____

13 運送；運載；搬運 _____

14 空氣　_____

15 籽；種子　_____

16 成長為……　_____

Daily Test 14 What Do Plants Need?

A Listen to the passage and fill in the blanks. 🎧 50

Have you ever _____ to grow a plant?

You probably realized that plants need many things to _____.

First, plants need _____.

Plants can get water from the ground or from the _____.

Without water, plants will _____.

Plants also need _____ from the soil.

The soil _____ many important nutrients that plants need to grow.

Plants need air and _____ as well.

Leaves help the plant _____ the air it needs.

The leaves also _____ _____ sunlight to make food for the plant.

Finally, plants need _____ to grow and to stay healthy.

As plants get bigger, they need more room to grow _____.

B Write the meaning of each word or phrase from Word List in English.

1	試圖；嘗試	_____	9	也；同樣地	_____
2	生長；發育	_____	10	讓……進入；接受；吸收	_____
3	大概；或許；很可能	_____	11	最後；終於	_____
4	領悟；了解；認識到	_____	12	空間	_____
5	雨	_____	13	健康的	_____
6	無；沒有；不	_____	14	變大	_____
7	（草木等）枯萎；凋謝	_____	15	房間	_____
8	包含；容納	_____	16	長大	_____

15 Where Do Animals Live?

A Listen to the passage and fill in the blanks.   🎧 51

Do you think polar bears could live in a _____?

How about _____?

Animals live in different _____.

The place where an animal lives is its _____.

Animals can have food and _____ safe in their habitat.

A forest habitat has many _____.

Animals like _____, squirrels, and rabbits live there.

A _____ gets rain almost every day and is hot all year.

Snakes, lizards, and _____ live there.

A desert is very dry and has lots of _____.

Small animals, like rats, scorpions, and _____, live there.

A grassland is covered with _____.

Zebras, giraffes, and _____ live there.

A _____ is a very cold and snowy place.

Polar bears and caribous live _____.

B Write the meaning of each word or phrase from Word List in English.

1 北極熊 _____

2 沙漠 _____

3 你認為……怎樣 _____

4 地方；地點；地區；位置 _____

5 棲息地 _____

6 鹿 _____

7 松鼠 _____

8 熱帶雨林 _____

9 蜥蜴 _____

10 鱷魚 _____

11 沙子 _____

12 老鼠 _____

13 蠍子 _____

14 蜘蛛 _____

15 草原 _____

16 草；牧草 _____

17 斑馬 _____

18 長頸鹿 _____

19 苔原；凍土地帶；凍原 _____

20 北美馴鹿 _____

16 Water Habitats

A Listen to the passage and fill in the blanks. 🎧 52

Water _____ most of the earth.

So there are many _____ habitats.

These include _____, lakes, rivers, and oceans.

Oceans are the earth's biggest _____.

An ocean is a very large body of _____ water.

There is a lot of _____ life in the oceans.

Some animals, like plankton, are so _____ that you can barely see them.

Others, such as _____, are the largest animals on the earth.

Ponds, lakes, and rivers have _____ water.

Many _____ live in fresh water, too.

How do fish _____ in the water?

Animals on land have _____ to breathe air.

But fish have _____.

Fish use gills to take in _____ from the water.

B Write the meaning of each word or phrase from Word List in English.

1 覆蓋 _____

2 包括；包含 _____

3 池塘 _____

4 鹹水；海水 _____

5 海底生物 _____

6 （總稱）浮游生物 _____

7 極小的；微小的 _____

8 僅僅；勉強；幾乎沒有 _____

9 鯨魚 _____

10 淡水 _____

11 呼吸；呼氣；吸氣 _____

12 肺；肺臟 _____

13 （魚）鰓 _____

14 氧氣 _____

17 Weather

A Listen to the passage and fill in the blanks. 🎧 53

Every day, when people wake up, they look _____.

What are they _____?

They are _____ the weather.

Weather _____ our daily lives a lot.

What is _____?

Weather is what the air outside is _____.

The weather can be sunny, cloudy, rainy, or _____.

It can change in a few _____ or day to day.

How can you _____ weather?

We use some _____ to measure the weather.

A thermometer measures _____.

Temperature shows how _____ or cold the air is.

We measure the temperature in units called _____.

Some tools measure _____ or rain.

A weather vane indicates the _____ of the wind.

A rain _____ is used to find out how much rain falls.

B Write the meaning of each word or phrase from Word List in English.

1 醒來；起床 _____

2 天氣 _____

3 影響；對……發生作用 _____

4 日常生活 _____

5 像；如 _____

6 陽光充足的；和煦的；暖和的 _____

7 多雲的；陰天的 _____

8 下雨的；多雨的 _____

9 雪的；下雪的；多雪的 _____

10 測量 _____

11 工具；器具；用具 _____

12 溫度計 _____

13 溫度；氣溫 _____

14 單位；單元 _____

15 度 _____

16 風向計 _____

17 顯示；指示；指出 _____

18 方向 _____

19 雨量計 _____

20 找出；發現；查明 _____

Daily Test 18 The Four Seasons

A Listen to the passage and fill in the blanks.   ♪ 54

In many places, the weather _____ with each season.

There are four _____: spring, summer, fall, and winter.

In spring, the weather gets _____.

Most plants begin to _____.

In some places, it rains a lot during _____.

In _____, the weather is usually very hot.

It is the _____ season of the year.

The days in summer are long, so there are many hours of _____.

When fall comes, the weather gets _____.

The leaves change _____ and fall off the trees.

Winter is the _____ season of the year.

In some places, it snows a lot _____ winter.

Also, the days in _____ are short.

So there are few hours of _____ during winter.

B Write the meaning of each word or phrase from Word List in English.

1 季節　_____
2 四季　_____
3 隨著……而改變　_____
4 變得更暖和　_____
5 下雨；降雨　_____
6 最溫暖的；最暖和的　_____
7 一天（24小時）；日　_____
8 秋天　_____
9 變得更涼爽　_____
10 從……落下　_____
11 雪；降雪　_____
12 日光；白晝　_____

19

19 What Can You See in the Sky?

A Listen to the passage and fill in the blanks. 🎧 55

On a clear night, go outside and _____ _____ in the sky.

You can _____ see many objects.

The biggest _____ in the night sky is the moon.

The moon is a huge ball of _____ that moves around Earth.

You can see _____ of tiny stars also.

Actually, a star is a huge ball of hot _____.

Stars look tiny because they are so _____ _____ from Earth.

Most stars can be _____ only at night.

In the daytime, the sunlight is so _____ that you cannot see them.

But they are _____ there.

During the day, you _____ see the sun.

Do you know that the sun is a _____?

It looks so bright and big because it is the _____ star to Earth.

B Write the meaning of each word or phrase from Word List in English.

1	明亮的；晴朗的		10	數以百計；許多
2	到外面		11	極小的；微小的
3	向上看；仰視		12	氣體
4	物體		13	（離……）很遠
5	夜空		14	白天；白晝
6	月亮；月球		15	如此……以至於……
7	龐大的；巨大的		16	明亮的；發亮的；晴朗的
8	球；球狀體		17	靜止的；不動的
9	圍繞……運動		18	最近的

20 What Causes Day and Night?

A Listen to the passage and fill in the blanks.   ⌒ 56

Each day, the sun seems to _____ in the morning and set at night.

But the sun is not really _____. Earth is moving.

Earth _____.

To rotate means to _____ around like a top.

It _____ 24 hours for Earth to rotate one time.

One _____ is one day.

Earth's rotation _____ day and night.

Earth is _____ like a ball.

As Earth rotates, there is sunlight where Earth _____ the sun.

That part of Earth has _____. The other side has nighttime.

As Earth rotates, the part that was light _____ away from the sun and

gets dark.

That part of Earth has _____.

The other _____ that was dark has daytime.

This pattern _____ every 24 hours.

B Write the meaning of each word or phrase from Word List in English.

1 看來好像；似乎 _____

2 （日、月等）上升；升起 _____

3 （日、月等）落；下沈 _____

4 確實；實際上 _____

5 移動；離開；前進 _____

6 旋轉；轉動 _____

7 （陀螺等）旋轉；（人、物）旋轉 _____

8 像；如 _____

9 陀螺 _____

10 需要；花費；佔用 _____

11 旋轉；（天體）自轉 _____

12 導致；使發生；引起 _____

13 成形；成型；形成 _____

14 面向；正對 _____

15 夜間 _____

16 轉過去 _____

17 變暗；變黑 _____

18 重複；重做 _____

21 Solids, Liquids, and Gases

A Listen to the passage and fill in the blanks. 🎧 57

Everything in the world is _____ _____ matter.

Air, water, and this book are all made of _____.

Matter has three _____.

They are solids, liquids, and _____.

A solid is a hard object that can be _____.

Only a _____ has a shape of its own.

Cars, books, rocks, and _____ are all solids.

Water is a _____.

A liquid does not have a shape of its _____.

It takes the shape of its _____.

Juice, milk, and _____ are all liquids.

_____ is made up of gases.

Like a liquid, a gas does not have _____ own shape.

It _____ all of the space of its container.

The air inside balloons, helium, and _____ is all gases.

B Write the meaning of each word or phrase from Word List in English.

1 由……製成 _____

2 物質 _____

3 形狀；外形 _____

4 固體 _____

5 液體 _____

6 氣體 _____

7 接觸；碰到 _____

8 自己的 _____

9 冰 _____

10 接受；採取；變成 _____

11 容器 _____

12 可樂 _____

13 由……組成 _____

14 裝滿；充滿 _____

15 氣球 _____

16 蒸氣；水蒸氣；水氣 _____

22 The Water Cycle

A Listen to the passage and fill in the blanks. 🎧 58

Water can be a solid, a _____, or a gas.

When water gets warm, it changes _____ a gas.

The gas is called _____ _____.

When water vapor gets cool, it _____ _____ into water.

Water can change into a solid ice when it _____.

This water _____ makes it rain or snow.

The sun _____ the water in the oceans and on land.

Some water _____ _____ water vapor.

As the water vapor _____ into the air, the temperature gets colder.

This _____ the water vapor turn back into water.

The water gathers in the sky in the form of _____.

Eventually, the clouds _____ their water.

In warm weather, the water _____ to Earth as rain.

In cold weather, the water falls _____ snow.

Then the water cycle begins _____.

B Write the meaning of each word or phrase from Word List in English.

1 改變為……；變化為…… _____

2 水蒸氣 _____

3 變回 _____

4 變成 _____

5 結冰；凝固 _____

6 把……加熱；變熱；發熱 _____

7 收集；召集；使聚集 _____

8 雲 _____

9 最後；終於 _____

10 釋放；解放 _____

11 降落；落下 _____

A Listen to the passage and fill in the blanks. 🎧59

Your body has many _____ parts.

All your parts work together to help you _____.

Let's learn about some of the _____ of your body.

Bones are the hard body parts _____ your body.

They _____ each body part to one another.

They _____ your body _____ and give the body its shape.

Bones also _____ many important parts inside your body.

There are more than _____ bones inside you.

All together, they form your _____ system.

Muscles are body parts that make you _____.

You use _____ to walk, run, and jump.

You even use your muscles to talk, eat, _____, and sing.

There are more than _____ muscles inside you.

Your _____ system is made up of these muscles.

B Write the meaning of each word or phrase from Word List in English.

1 一部分；部分 _____

2 活；活著 _____

3 體系；系統 _____

4 骨；骨頭 _____

5 硬的；堅固的 _____

6 內部；裡面 _____

7 連接；連結 _____

8 托住；支撐 _____

9 防衛；保護 _____

10 形成；構成；塑造 _____

11 骨骼的 _____

12 骨骼系統 _____

13 肌肉 _____

14 笑；嘲笑 _____

15 肌肉的 _____

16 肌肉系統 _____

24 The Systems of Your Body

A Listen to the passage and fill in the blanks.　　🎧 60

Let's _____ more about the systems of your body.

You breathe using your _____ system.

Your mouth and _____ take in oxygen from the air.

Then, the oxygen goes into your lungs and moves through your _____.

Blood _____ in your body through your circulatory system.

It is made up of your heart and blood _____.

Your heart _____ blood through blood vessels.

Blood vessels are small _____.

They carry blood from your _____ to every part of your body.

Your body gets _____ from the food you eat.

When you eat, your digestive system _____ _____ the food.

This _____ your body get energy to do things.

B Write the meaning of each word or phrase from Word List in English.

1　呼吸；呼氣；吸氣　_____

2　呼吸的　_____

3　呼吸系統　_____

4　讓……進入；接受　_____

5　通過　_____

6　血；血液　_____

7　（使）循環　_____

8　循環上的　_____

9　血液循環系統　_____

10　由……構成　_____

11　心臟　_____

12　血管　_____

13　把某物從某物抽入、抽出、抽上去　_____

14　管；筒　_____

15　活力；精力　_____

16　消化的；助消化的　_____

17　消化系統　_____

18　分解　_____

25 Shapes and Figures

A Listen to the passage and fill in the blanks. 🎧 61

Can you name these _____?

△ ▭ ▢ ○

A shape with three sides is called a _____.

A rectangle has four _____.

A square has four sides of equal _____.

A circle is _____ and has no sides.

These shapes are called flat shapes or plane _____.

A figure is a _____ shape.

There are many _____ shapes, too.

A _____ is a solid-shaped circle.

A _____ is a solid-shaped square.

Cones, pyramids, and _____ are also solid shapes.

Everywhere you _____, you can see solid shapes and figures.

They are in _____ and in everyday objects.

Look _____ your home or school for example.

What figures do you _____?

B Write the meaning of each word or phrase from Word List in English.

1	形狀	13	平面圖形
2	邊	14	規則的;正規的
3	三角形	15	立體;立體的
4	矩形;長方形	16	立體形狀
5	正方形;方形物;方塊	17	球;球體;球形;球面
6	相等的;相當的;均等的	18	立體形狀的
7	（距離、尺寸的）長度	19	立方體;立方形物體
8	圓;圓圈	20	圓錐體;圓錐形
9	平的;平坦的	21	三角錐（體）
10	平面形狀	22	圓柱;圓筒;圓柱狀物
11	平面	23	立體圖形
12	圖形	24	四下觀望;環顧四周

26 What Am I?

A Listen to the passage and fill in the blanks. 🎧 62

Let me tell you about _____.

I have six _____.

A face is a flat _____ of a solid figure.

So I am a _____ figure.

My faces _____ at various points.

An edge is formed _____ two of my faces meet.

I have many _____.

I have _____ of them.

My faces also meet at different _____.

A vertex is a _____ where three or more edges meet.

I have _____ vertices.

Now do you _____ what I am?

I'm a _____!

B Write the meaning of each word or phrase from Word List in English.

1 讓；允許   _____
2 我自己   _____
3 面   _____
4 面；表面   _____
5 平面   _____
6 相交；交叉   _____

7 不同的；各種各樣的；形形色色的 _____
8 點   _____
9 邊   _____
10 （物體）成形；被形成 _____
11 頂點   _____
12 立方體；立方形物體 _____

27 Counting Numbers

A Listen to the passage and fill in the blanks. 🎧 63

Let's _____ from 1 to 100.

One, two, three, four, five. Six, seven, _____, nine, ten.

What about the _____ ten numbers?

Eleven, twelve, thirteen, fourteen, _____.

Sixteen, seventeen, eighteen, nineteen, _____.

How do we count _____ than twenty?

First, we need to know these _____:

Thirty, forty, fifty, sixty, seventy, eighty, and _____.

After these words, just _____ a number from 1 to 9.

Now you can count to _____ (one hundred).

Let's practice counting by _____: 10, 20, 30, 40, 50, 60, 70, 80, 90.

Also, practice counting _____: 49, 48, 47, and so on.

We sometimes use _____ numbers.

We use these numbers to tell the _____ or position of something.

The first ten are first, second, _____, fourth, fifth.

Sixth, seventh, eighth, ninth, and _____.

_____ for first, second, and third, ordinal numbers end in "th."

B Write the meaning of each word or phrase from Word List in English.

1	計算；數	_____	7	有時；間或
2	比……高	_____	8	序數
3	需要；有……必要	_____	9	順序
4	添加；增加	_____	10	位置；地點；方位
5	數十進位；從十數到一百	_____	11	除了……以外
6	倒數	_____	12	以……為結果

28 Comparing Numbers

A Listen to the passage and fill in the blanks. 🎧 64

Let's compare the _____ of numbers.

On a number line, a number that comes after another number is always

1 _____.

For example, 6 is 1 more _____ 5.

So we can say, "6 is _____ than 5."

Or we can _____ it like this: 6 > 5.

The sign > _____ "is greater than."

On a number line, a number that comes _____ another number is always

1 less.

For example, 3 is 1 _____ than 4.

So we can say, "3 is less _____ 4," or 3 < 4.

The _____ < means "is less than."

Sometimes, two numbers have the _____ value.

For example, "3 is _____ to 3."

We can write it _____ this: 3 = 3.

The sign = means "is equal to" or "is the same _____."

B Write the meaning of each word or phrase from Word List in English.

1 比較　　_____

2 值；數值　_____

3 例子；樣本　_____

4 例如；舉例來說　_____

5 數列　　_____

6 更多的　　_____

7 大於　　_____

8 符號　　_____

9 較小的；較少的　_____

10 小於　　_____

11 等於　　_____

12 與⋯⋯相同；與⋯⋯相等　_____

29 Being a Good Writer

A Listen to the passage and fill in the blanks.

A good writer uses good _____ and punctuation.

Grammar is the rules of a _____.

When you write a sentence, use the _____ words and expressions.

Also, use proper punctuation marks to show where the _____ stops.

Here are a few rules for _____.

Capitalization:

1. Use a _____ letter at the beginning of a sentence.

2. The _____ "I" is always a capital letter.

3. The names of people or special places should _____ with a capital letter.

4. Capitalize the names of the days of the week, _____, and holidays.

Punctuation:

1. Use a _____ to end a sentence.

2. All questions need a question _____.

3. To show surprise or excitement, use an _____ point.

4. Use a _____ between each person, place, thing, or phrase in a list.

B Write the meaning of each word or phrase from Word List in English.

1 作者；作家；記者；撰稿人 _____

2 文法 _____

3 標點法；標點 _____

4 語言；語言文字 _____

5 句子 _____

6 正確的；對的 _____

7 表達；措辭；詞句 _____

8 適合的；適當的；恰當的 _____

9 標點符號 _____

10 書寫；寫作；書面形式 _____

11 大寫 _____

12 大寫字母 _____

13 在……的開頭 _____

14 以大寫字母書寫 _____

15 問號 _____

16 驚奇；詫異 _____

17 興奮 _____

18 驚嘆號 _____

19 逗號 _____

20 片語；詞組 _____

30 Writing Friendly Letters

A Listen to the passage and fill in the blanks. 🎧66

August 5, _____

Dear _____,

How are you _____?
Everything is _____ with me.

I am having a great summer _____ my family.
We _____ at Palm Beach for one week.
I went _____ and fishing.
One day, we even did some _____!

How is your summer _____ going?
School is going to begin in two _____.
I'll see you in class _____.

Yours _____,
Tom

B Write the meaning of each word or phrase from Word List in English.

1 友好的；親切的 _____

2 友善的信 _____

3 （信頭稱謂）親愛的；尊敬的 _____

4 停留在 _____

5 釣魚 _____

6 浮潛 _____

7 暑假 _____

8 將要…… _____

9 在……裡；在……上 _____

10 真誠地；忠實地 _____

11 問候語 _____

12 （文章、書籍等的）正文；主要部分 _____

13 （演講或書信的）結尾辭 _____

14 忘記；忽略 _____

31 Aesop's Fables

A Listen to the passage and fill in the blanks. ⌒67

A long time ago, a man lived on the _____ island of Samos.

His name was Aesop, and he was a _____.

But he was also a great _____.

Aesop often _____ _____ stories to tell people.

His stories were called _____.

A fable is a short story that _____ people a lesson.

Animals are often the main _____.

The animals talk and act like _____.

At the end of the fable, Aesop always tells the _____ a lesson.

The lesson is called the _____ of the story.

Aesop wrote many _____ fables.

"The _____ and the Grasshopper" is one of them.

"The _____ and the Hare" is also very popular.

Today, both young and old people _____ reading Aesop's fables.

B Write the meaning of each word or phrase from Word List in English.

1 希臘人；希臘語 _____
2 奴隸 _____
3 說故事的人；作家 _____
4 編造；虛構 _____
5 寓言；虛構的故事；傳說；神話 _____
6 教訓；訓誡 _____
7 主要的；最重要的 _____
8 （小說、戲劇等的）人物；角色 _____
9 在……的末尾 _____

10 讀者；愛好閱讀者 _____
11 （寓言等的）寓意 _____
12 著名的；出名的 _____
13 螞蟻 _____
14 蚱蜢 _____
15 陸龜；龜；烏龜 _____
16 野兔 _____
17 廣為流傳的；流行的 _____
18 欣賞；享受；喜愛 _____

32 The Ant and the Grasshopper

A Listen to the passage and fill in the blanks. 🎧 68

An ant and a grasshopper once lived in the same _____.

Every day, the ant worked hard and _____ food for winter.

But the grasshopper just _____ and sang all summer long.

Summer changed to fall, and the weather became _____.

The ant started working even _____ than before.

But the grasshopper _____ played and played.

One day, the first snow _____.

The ant went inside and ate a nice, warm _____.

Meanwhile, the grasshopper started _____ from the cold.

"I'm cold and _____. What shall I do?" he said.

When spring came, the weather became _____.

So the ant went _____.

But the ant never saw the _____ again.

Moral: Don't forget to _____ for bad times even during good times.

B Write the meaning of each word or phrase from Word List in English.

1 昔日；曾經 _____
2 原野；田地；（廣闊的一大片）地 _____
3 收集；採集 _____
4 玩耍；遊戲；戲弄 _____
5 歌唱 _____
6 始終；一整個…… _____
7 （用於比較級前）甚至更；還 _____

8 還；仍舊 _____
9 落下；跌倒 _____
10 膳食；一餐 _____
11 其間；同時 _____
12 發抖 _____
13 為……做準備 _____
14 倒楣；不愉快的生活；焦慮不安的生活
   _____

33 Kinds of Paintings

A Listen to the passage and fill in the blanks. 🎧 69

Artists create many different kinds of _____.

Some _____ like to paint landscapes.

The most important thing in a landscape is the _____.

It often _____ the land, the trees, the sky, lakes, and rivers.

The weather, season, and time of the day are also very _____.

Some artists like to _____ still lifes.

The objects in a still life do not _____.

That is why it is called a _____ _____.

To paint a still life, an artist has to prepare the _____ to paint.

Still lifes often include _____, flowers, and other small objects.

Paintings of people are other _____ works.

A painting of a person is called a _____.

A _____ is a portrait of the artist himself.

B Write the meaning of each word or phrase from Word List in English.

1 藝術家;美術家(尤指畫家) _____
2 創造;創作;設計 _____
3 種類 _____
4 繪畫;繪畫藝術;畫法 _____
5 畫;繪畫 _____
6 風景;風景畫 _____
7 景色;景物 _____

8 一天特定時段 _____
9 靜物畫 _____
10 常見的;一般的 _____
11 著作;作品 _____
12 肖像;人像 _____
13 自畫像 _____
14 他自己;他本人 _____

34 Painting and Drawing Materials

A Listen to the passage and fill in the blanks. 🎧70

Artists need special _____ to make their pictures.

They need _____ materials, paints, brushes, a canvas, and an easel.

There are several kinds of _____ .

Oil paints are popular with many _____ .

Oil paints produce rich and _____ colors on the pictures.

Other artists prefer to use _____ and finger paints.

Watercolor pictures are often very _____ .

Finger paints produce _____ and fun pictures.

There are many _____ of drawing materials.

Of course, some artists just use simple _____ .

But others use color pencils to _____ their pictures.

Some prefer _____, which also come in many colors.

And a few artists draw pictures with _____ .

All of these drawing materials can produce great _____ .

B Write the meaning of each word or phrase from Word List in English.

1 材料；原料　　_____

2 畫；畫像；圖片；照片　_____

3 描繪；素描；圖畫　_____

4 顏料　　_____

5 毛筆；畫筆　_____

6 油畫布；油畫　_____

7 畫架；黑板架　_____

8 幾個的；數個的　_____

9 油畫顏料　_____

10 畫家　　_____

11 製造；創作　_____

12 （顏色）濃豔的　_____

13 （色彩、光線等）鮮豔的；鮮明的；強烈的

　　_____

14 偏好；更喜歡　_____

15 水彩；水彩顏料　_____

16 指畫用的顏料　_____

17 唯一的；獨一無二的；獨特的　_____

18 使明亮；使閃亮　_____

19 蠟筆　　_____

20 （畫木炭畫的）炭條；炭筆　_____

35 Musical Instruments

A Listen to the passage and fill in the blanks. ∩ 71

There are different kinds of _____ instruments.

Let's meet the string _____.

Can you name some instruments with _____?

The violin? The cello? How about the _____?

You usually use _____ to play string instruments.

But sometimes you _____ the strings with your fingers.

Let's meet the _____ family.

These include the drum, _____, and tambourine.

Percussion instruments are fun to _____.

You hit them or shake them with your hands or a _____.

The _____ are some other common instruments.

Some woodwinds are the clarinet, _____, and oboe.

Musicians play the woodwinds by _____ air into them.

Musicians also blow into _____ instruments.

The trumpet and _____ are two of them.

The piano and organ are _____ instruments.

You can play keyboard instruments by using your _____.

B Write the meaning of each word or phrase from Word List in English.

1 樂器 _____

2 （樂器等的）弦 _____

3 弦樂器 _____

4 琴弓 _____

5 演奏；彈奏；吹奏 _____

6 撥；彈 _____

7 打擊樂器 _____

8 木琴 _____

9 搖；搖動；震動 _____

10 木棒 _____

11 木管樂器 _____

12 吹奏 _____

13 銅管樂器 _____

14 鍵盤樂器 _____

36 The Orchestra

A Listen to the passage and fill in the blanks. 🎧 72

Have you ever attended a _____?

Or have you ever watched an orchestra on _____?

All of the musical instruments come together in an _____.

String, percussion, woodwind, brass, and keyboard instruments

_____ _____ an orchestra.

The musicians all play _____, and they make beautiful music.

The conductor _____ the orchestra.

He or she stands in front of the orchestra and _____ the music.

The _____ makes sure that all the members do their jobs at the

right time.

This lets them play in _____.

Most orchestras play _____ music.

They might play _____ by Mozart or Bach.

But some play _____ or pop music as well.

B Write the meaning of each word or phrase from Word List in English.

1	出席；參加	_____
2	音樂會；演奏會	_____
3	管弦樂隊	_____
4	組成	_____
5	指揮家	_____
6	領導；指揮；率領	_____
7	站立；站著	_____
8	在⋯⋯的前面	_____

9	指揮	_____
10	設法確保；確定	_____
11	做某人的工作	_____
12	在正確時刻	_____
13	和諧；協調；調和	_____
14	古典樂	_____
15	歌劇	_____
16	流行音樂	_____

MEMO